Dedication

To "Auntie" Hulda Telker (1926-2023)

Acknowledgement

As always, a group of people deserve credit for helping mold my manuscripts. Brian Johnson is my Two Harbors muse who fills my head with plots, locations, and characters. Without his persistent nudging, the Whistling Pines series wouldn't exist. I turn to Brian when the characters stop speaking to me. When I tell him I'm stuck, he responds with pages of zany ideas that somehow fit into the plot and get my creative juices flowing.

Julie reads the first completed draft of each book, offering opinions and correcting medical situations and terminology. Deanna Wilson reads isolated chapters and out-of-context fragments as I write them, correcting errors and urging me on. She's also my police and horse consultant. Larry Fralich, a Silver Bay volunteer fireman and friend, brainstormed with me about Lake Superior's North Shore, hunting, fishing, and old guns, leading to some of the key elements of this plot.

Mike Westfall, Clem MacIlravie, Marybeth Johnson, and Fran Brozo read beta drafts, and offered opinions that steered me to this final version. Anne Flagge, Warren Wasecha, and Natalie Lund proofread and removed typos and grammatical errors.

Many thanks to Jude Pittman of BWL for her editorial help and support.

Whistling Fireman

Whistling Pines Book 8

Dean L. Hovey

Print ISBNs
Amazon Print 9780228627258
Ingram Spark Print 9780228627265
Barnes &Noble Print 9780228627272

Copyright 2023 by Dean Hovey
Cover art by Michelle Lee

This book is a work of fiction, a product of the author's imagination. Any resemblance to actual events, people, or places is coincidental and unintended. Some Two Harbors businesses are used fictionally.

Table of Contents

Prologue

Flames were already licking the eaves of Oldham's Bait Shop when the first Two Harbors fire truck's siren whined. It would take the first volunteer firemen at least another five minutes to arrive at the scene, located a mile north of the station. It would then take the firemen another two minutes to unroll hoses and spray water onto the flames. Although he was neither a mathematician, nor a chemist, the arsonist knew the intensity of the fire would double every two minutes. By the time the firefighters arrived, there would be little they could do except keep the fire from igniting the bulk propane tank in the driveway.

From the hill above, the arsonist watched as the flames crept higher and grew brighter. Windows exploded and flames burst out of the open back door. The building was already a total loss, and the volunteer firemen's slow response would guarantee that any evidence of the crime would be consumed before the flames were doused.

Flashing blue and red lights raced out of town. The Two Harbor's police officer responding to the 911 call arrived on the scene minutes ahead of the fire trucks. *Like the cop will be able to do anything but divert the rubberneckers until the firemen arrive*, the arsonist thought.

A man in a passing car stopped to snap photos of the fire as the police arrived. "Hah!" the arsonist said, "If you hang around, the cops will suspect that you're the one who lit the fire!"

A second car stopped, its driver stepping out with his cell phone, probably calling his buddies to report that they'd have to buy their bait elsewhere. The lone policeman parked on the road. He looked skyward at the flames now arching higher than the building's roof. Apparently assuming there was no one to be saved, and that the use of the tiny fire extinguisher in his trunk would be useless, he took the names of the two gawkers, then shooed them away as the first fire truck appeared around the bend of the road.

The fire chief, known as Sparky to the locals, was the first person out of the truck. He took in the enormity of the conflagration and then directed the other three firemen as they pulled a small hose off a reel. It was a futile gesture, but one of the firemen directed the small stream of water into the flames where the display window had been.

"They must feel like they were making an effort," the arsonist whispered to himself.

The other two firemen wrestled a larger hose from the back of the truck and pulled it toward a fire hydrant while Sparky attached the other end to a fitting on the side of the truck. Moments later, as they were directing water from a three-inch hose into the front door as the second fire truck pulled into the bait shop parking lot. More sirens wailed as engines from surrounding communities responded to Sparky's call for assistance. Firemen and trucks from the Silver Bay, Brimson, and Northstar fire departments rushed to the scene.

The arsonist watched their futile efforts with glee as the third and fourth fire trucks arrived on the scene. "The puny amount of water you're pouring into that building won't douse the flames. You might as well just wait for the contents to burn themselves out."

Feeling exposed as the flames crept higher and lit the hill behind the building, the arsonist slipped over the crest behind him and walked through the woods using a flashlight to thread his way through the underbrush. A mile from the fire, he climbed into his rusty pickup parked on a deserted township road. He envisioned the chaotic scene on the other side of the hill. Pausing briefly at a stop sign to let yet another fire truck pass, he smiled as he watched the plume of dark smoke climb toward the sliver of moon in the cloudless sky.

Chapter 1

I'm Peter Rogers, the recreation director for Whistling Pines Senior Residence and I'm often called upon to do a variety of things outside what most people consider to be a *normal* recreation director's job description. One of those duties is to monitor the rumor mill, which I do by having coffee with the residents. Another is to organize the group of residents who decorate the inside of the building for each holiday. I was accomplishing both of those functions by watching residents cutting pumpkin shapes from orange craft paper. A few residents taped paper witches riding brooms to the dining room windows. A third group assembled decorations for the entryway from gourds and corn stalks.

"Bah!" Hulda Packer exclaimed as she pushed her walker into the dining room. "Halloween is a made-up holiday, like minister's day."

I turned in my chair, curious about her comment. "I've never heard of minister's day, Hulda. When is that celebrated?" I asked as she approached my table wearing her usual frown.

Glaring at me, Hulda said, "It's on the first Sunday of Paracost."

Knowing that Hulda twisted things, I tried to correct her. "Do you mean Pentecost?"

Not a person who took corrections well, Hulda squared herself, facing me. "If I'd meant Pentecost, I would've said, Pentecost."

"When is Paracost?" I asked as more people stopped whatever they were doing to listen to Hulda's answer, delivered in an outdoor voice.

Momentarily stumped, Hulda clicked her dentures while she dreamt up an answer. "Paracost means between ribs. It's the day that God removed Adam's rib to create Eve. You know, on the sixth day of creation. It's always celebrated on the sixth Saturday of the sixth month."

A titter of laughter arose as people calculated that there could never be a sixth Saturday in June. "What?" Hulda said, giving individual people her stink-eye look. "It's like the 29th of February. It only comes around every six years."

Trying to end the conversation before Hulda exploded in a tirade, I stood and offered her my chair. "Have a seat. I'll get you a cup of coffee."

I glanced at my tablemates, Mary Gilbert, Karla Telker, and Kathy Christensen, who were all displeased with the prospect of Hulda joining their quiet, sane discussion as they cut pumpkin shapes from orange construction paper. Karla looked at me and rolled her eyes before smiling and adding, "Hulda, I could get you a caramel roll to go with the coffee."

Hulda glared at Karla. "The caramel pulls off my dentures. I'll pass." Pushing her walker in a wide U-turn, Hulda shoved her way past two women who were stringing a row of paper ghosts over the dining room entrance.

Kathy, who was sweet, tolerant, and a little sassy, leaned toward me as I sat down. "I understand that you're trying to be the diplomat, but offering a chair at our table to Hulda is inhumane."

"It's not that bad, Kathy."

Mary laughed. "You're devious. You'd give her your chair, leaving us to deal with Hulda's insanity, while you wander back to your office."

"Karla and Hulda had both been teachers," I countered. "They have so much in common."

Karla leaned forward and tapped her fingertip on the table. "Hulda taught when it was acceptable to rap an unruly child's knuckles with a wooden ruler."

Mary added, "That was also before Hulda's dementia."

Our conversation was interrupted when Kerry Stone, the Two Harbors police chief, walked into the dining room. His gaze quickly went to me. He wiggled a finger, beckoning me to the lobby.

Kathy grabbed my arm, her eyes sparkling. "You're probably going to be ticketed for your inhumane treatment of senior citizens."

Kerry walked to the atrium outside the dining room as I weaved through tables, greeting residents while trying not to get drawn into a discussion. I met the chief standing alongside the aviary. "What's up?"

"Did you hear about last night's fire at Oldham's Bait Shop?"

"I didn't listen to the news this morning and it hasn't been a topic of discussion in the dining room."

Kerry smiled with the unscarred side of his face; the left side having been badly burned when he served in Iraq, it was covered with pink scar tissue and skin grafts that were frozen in place. "It's hard to believe that the Whistling Pines rumor mill wasn't buzzing about the arson fire."

"Arson?"

"There were melted plastic gas cans in the store's display area and office. It appears that the fire originated in two places."

"How badly was the building damaged?"

"A passing semi driver said it was a total loss. The flames were licking the outside of the building when he drove past. By the time the fire department arrived, all they could do was pump water into the building and keep the bulk propane tank from exploding."

"Wow!"

Kerry leaned close to me and lowered his voice. "We found a body in the storeroom."

"Were you able to identify the remains?"

"Not yet. We spoke with the owner when we notified him of the fire, so we know it wasn't Bud Oldham. He'd locked up at six o'clock, and he's sure there wasn't anyone inside the building then."

"Is Bud a suspect?" I asked.

Kerry took a moment before answering. "Bud was bowling when the fire started."

"So, he's not a suspect."

Kerry wrinkled his nose. "I'd say no, but there have been three other arson fires in small businesses in the past decade. All of the businesses were struggling, and all the owners had rock solid alibis."

"Insurance fraud?"

"Talk to your local historians. They might have heard something that never made it into the police investigations."

"You do realize that their fading memories lead them to enhance their recall of events."

"Yes. On the other hand, you've got over a hundred people with decades of Two Harbors history in their brains. There are certainly enough threads of reality locked in their collective memories."

Chuckling, I replied, "Those locks tend to be a little rusty."

Kerry straightened up and looked toward the front entrance. "I'm trying to decide if I've got enough time to patrol town before the Chamber of Commerce meeting at Judy's."

"What Chamber of Commerce meeting?"

Kerry smiled. "The one where we plan the Halloween Festival."

"What Halloween Festival?" I asked.

Kerry put his hand on my arm and leaned close. "The one on Halloween. I'll see you at 10:00 o'clock."

"I don't know anything about a Halloween Festival meeting!" I called out to Kerry's back as he walked to the front door.

"It's at Judy's. Check your email!"

After rushing back to my office while fending off people trying to ask questions about activities, or just to chat, I entered my password and opened my email. The problem with not receiving a lot of meaningful emails is that I tend to ignore whole blocks of spam and insurance offers. Two emails down in my unread mail file was a note from Meg Cochran, the Chamber of Commerce chairperson, inviting the membership to a planning meeting.

The closing line read, "Please bring ideas for activities that will attract families."

Checking the computer clock, I saw that it was already 9:43. I briefly considered blowing off the meeting, then reconsidered. The last time I'd missed a planning meeting, Kerry volunteered me to chair the roadside trash pick-up committee. I quickly learned that my attendance was mandatory.

* * *

Judy's Café was half full when I arrived. Kerry sat at his usual spot in the back, where he could watch the crowd and front door. By the time I got past the tables filled with businesspeople, Kerry had already poured a mug of coffee for me.

"What's your suggested activity?" he asked.

"I'm not falling for that again," I replied as I draped my jacket over the back of the chair next to Kerry. "The last time I shared an idea ahead of the meeting, you stood up and suggested it without giving me credit."

Kerry raised his unscarred eyebrow. "Who, me?"

"Yes, you," I replied as I sat.

Judy, the café's owner, appeared carrying a tray covered with slices of pie and pastries. "The apple pie just came out of the oven," she announced, offering a choice of goodies as she passed among the tables.

Kerry took a cinnamon roll, and I chose a piece of still-steaming apple pie. After peeling off a corner of the sticky roll with a fork, Kerry smiled. "This almost makes the meeting worthwhile."

I tried to give him a stink-eye, but it apparently looked more like I had a nervous tic. "The last time I skipped a meeting, someone volunteered me to chair a committee."

Overhearing our conversation while passing, Meg stopped. "Kerry and I discussed what a great strategy that was to get people to attend meetings."

"I want to propose an agenda item suggesting that people not in attendance can't be stuck with assignments," I said.

"Huh," Meg said. "I don't remember seeing that on the agenda." She walked away before I could protest.

"Do you have any ideas?" I asked, sampling a slice of cinnamon coated apple that crunched when I bit into it.

"I think we should have a costume contest," Kerry replied, peeling off more of his cinnamon roll.

"This being a Halloween festival, I expect a dozen people are ready to offer that suggestion."

Meg tapped her water glass with a spoon to get everyone's attention. Before all the conversations stopped, Kerry stood and cleared his throat. "I suggest we have a costume contest as part of the festival."

Meg looked mildly surprised but smiled. "I'm pleased that at least one person came prepared with a suggestion. Thank you, Chief Stone."

"That was..." I paused, unable to come up with the proper adjective.

"Inspired," Kerry said as he settled into his chair.

"I think devious would be more appropriate," I whispered.

Meg saw our exchange and pointed. "I just saw Peter Rogers whispering an idea to the Chief. What's your suggestion, Peter?"

I froze like the child caught whispering in class. My mind raced. "I think we should have a pumpkin theme. I'm sure there are a dozen bakers who would submit their favorite pumpkin pie recipes for judging."

"Excellent suggestion, Peter! We can set up tables in the park," Meg said as she made a note. "Who would you suggest as a third judge?"

"Third judge?" I asked.

Meg nodded. "In addition to you and Chief Stone."

Pastor Vogel, from the Svenska Gotter Church raised his hand. "My daughter Sherry will be the third judge. She knows Peter and Kerry."

Kerry leaned close. "You're turning red."

"Sherry Vogel was the nude model at the art studio."

"Yeah, I heard Pastor Vogel was making her do community service as penance for her brief experience as a nude model for the Whistling Pines art class. I suspect he has suggested pairing her with us because he feels we're harmless."

Meg saw us talking and pointed to me. "Did you have another suggestion, Peter?"

"No, I was just commenting on what a great judge Sherry Vogel will make."

A male voice from somewhere near the door spoke in a stage whisper, "I've heard she's quite good at providing artistic inspiration."

Ignoring that comment, Meg accepted suggestions for a pumpkin carving contest, and separate children's and adult costume contests.

Clifford Berggren, the owner of the auto repair center, had never said a word in any previous meeting, so everyone was amazed when he raised his hand. "I'd like to build a pumpkin cannon. If we had a couple of entrants, we could have a contest to see whose cannon shoots the farthest."

Meg hesitated. "Are you talking about a town square military cannon using gunpowder, Cliff?"

"Naw. I've seen a couple of designs using compressed air or propane. I'd like to make one that uses compressed air. I'll bet something like that could shoot a pumpkin fifty yards."

Burt Halstrom, the machine shop owner, stood up. "You're on, Cliff. I'll make a propane version. We can shoot them on the football field. It's already got yardage markers to measure how far the pumpkins fly."

"Great suggestions!" Meg said as she made notes. "A competition like that would draw a crowd."

People started to chatter about the pumpkin cannon idea when a quiet voice said, "Can we have gambling?"

Meg shushed the crowd. "Say that again, Brandi."

Brandi Birch, owner of the Green Acres Alpaca Farm, stood up. "I asked if we could have gambling."

Meg looked at Kerry, who shrugged, then said, "I think charitable gambling would be okay. What did you have in mind?"

"We could use chalk to mark Owens Park into squares. I'll bring in a couple of my alpacas, and people can bet on which square they think the alpacas will poop in. There could be first and second place. The winners would each get a share of the money collected from the bets. The profit could be given to a charity of our choice."

"Won't they just walk into the middle and stand over one square?" Meg asked.

"They get nervous around strangers and pace. I think they'll move around quite a bit."

Kerry stood, looking concerned. "I don't want a bunch of controversy because the alpaca pies splatter in more than one square."

Brandi shook her head. "Alpacas don't make cow pies. Their poop is more like clumps of black beans. It'll be pretty evident which square they've made their deposit in."

Meg looked around. "Are there any other poop-related questions?" With no further discussion, Meg asked, "Does anyone else have another suggested activity?"

"Could we get someone to sell hot chocolate?" Brandi asked. "It's cold at the end of October."

Meg made a note. "I've got the names of the food truck vendors from the Pirate Festival. I'll see if any of them are interested in selling hot beverages for a Halloween festival."

Sparky, at the table next to us, stood up. "The firemen voted to move their annual Booya from November to the Halloween festival. We'll set up behind the bandstand if that's okay?"

Meg looked around the room. "It sounds good to me. Does anyone disagree?"

Kerry whispered, "What the hell is Booya?"

Sparky overheard him and explained, "Booya is a traditional Northwoods fall stew. We cook it in Oliver Holstad's cauldron and stir it with a canoe paddle."

Someone on the other side of us cleared his throat. "Booya is a chance for all the hunters and fishermen to clean out the frost-burned game they've got buried in their freezers."

Sparky frowned. "No way! There's a well-guarded secret Booya recipe that uses some wild game but also includes pork, vegetables, and potatoes. People come from miles around just to buy a bowl of fire department Booya. Some people even bring thermoses so they can bring Booya home to eat later."

I looked at Kerry, who'd clenched his eyes shut. "What's the matter?"

"Freezer burned wild game stew, cooked outside, in an open cauldron, stirred with a canoe paddle. What could go wrong with that?"

"No one will force you to eat any," I whispered.

"I'm more concerned about how many cases of food poisoning we'll have."

Several chamber members were smiling and nodding as they discussed their more positive memories of Booya.

Kerry hung back as the crowd left Judy's. Meg joined us as she packed her notes into a shoulder bag. "What's the matter, Chief? You look concerned."

"Something about cooking Booya in a big old pot near the alpaca pooping contest bothers me."

"The gambling?" I asked.

Kerry shook his head. "I just have this bad feeling about alpaca poop and wild game stew."

"I doubt Brandi would've suggested it if she thought it would cause any problems," Meg said.

"And the firemen cooking up wild game stew in an open outdoor pot doesn't scream food poisoning to you?"

"Kerry, the firemen have served Booya for as long as I can remember, and there's never been a case of food poisoning."

"I spent enough years in the Army to know that it's the unexpected that bites you in the butt. The Army even has an acronym for it. SNAFU."

"That's an acronym?" Meg asked.

I nodded. "Situation Normal; All Fouled Up."

Meg got a sly grin. "I bet the Army uses a different F word."

Kerry nodded. "Usually."

Meg looked at me, expecting a response.

"I was in the Navy. Sailors aren't as crude as soldiers."

Laughing, Meg replied, "Like I believe that."

Chapter 2

With Halloween approaching, I considered activities to entertain my Whistling Pines residents. The obvious activity would've been pumpkin carving, but knives in the shaky hands of senior citizens was a showstopper. I typed up an announcement for a Jack-o-lantern painting session, then sat back, trying to envision how I'd acquire dozens of pumpkins on my limited recreation budget and what paint we'd use.

"Hi, Doc," Brian Johnson said as he sat, uninvited, in my guest chair. "Why do bears hibernate?" When I didn't immediately respond, he said, "Because it's cheaper than flying to Florida."

I groaned, which broadened Brian's cherubic smile. "What brings you to Whistling Pines, Brian?"

"I heard that you're arranging the town's Halloween festival."

"I'm afraid your source is wrong. I'm on the Chamber of Commerce, but I'm not the arranger."

"That's too bad. I was hoping you'd consider donating the fundraiser proceeds to the bandshell reconstruction committee."

"The band did their own fundraising."

"I'm afraid they've lost steam now that the summer concert season has passed."

"How much are they short of their goal?"

Brian frowned, "The last I heard, they'd raised about half of what they needed. The conductor told me they've got enough money to cover the band shell demolition, but not construction."

"They can make a hole in the ground, but they can't fill it."

"That sums it up pretty well."

"Maybe the firemen will donate some of the Booya proceeds to the bandshell fundraiser."

"I'm not sure, but they seem to have financial needs within the department. You know, the kind of things the city doesn't cover in their fire department budget."

"I can't imagine the city doesn't cover all their needs. It's not like they'll be able to buy a new fire truck with the Booya profits."

"They're kind of elusive whenever I've asked about the Booya profits. I'm always left with the feeling they've used the money for their Christmas party, or something."

"I'm sure they have to reconcile the profit and use it for something more civic-minded than a fireman's Christmas party."

Brian's eyes drifted to my computer. "You're getting ready for pumpkin carving?"

"We paint pumpkins. It's lower risk than handing out knives to little old ladies with shaky hands." I paused. "Do you know where I could get a few dozen pumpkins for next to nothing?"

"Kyle Peterson grows pumpkins and always has hundreds left over after Halloween sales. I bet he'd make you a deal on the misshapen and puny ones. They never sell."

I made a note.

"Are you planning to make sauerkraut, too?"

"Um, no. Why would we make sauerkraut?"

"It was just a thought. Kyle grows cabbage. He would probably make you a deal on second-quality cabbage, too." Brian stood. "Think about the bandshell fundraiser."

"You need to talk to Meg. She's the chairperson."

After taking a step toward my door, Brian turned. "What do you get when you cross a vampire with a teacher?"

"I can't imagine."

"Lots of blood tests."

My groan only egged Brian on. "What do you call a zombie door-to-door salesman? A dead ringer."

Rather than offering the encouragement of a groan, I rolled my eyes.

"You'd better write those down for your son."

Brian left and I pulled a sheet of paper from the printer and wrote down the Halloween jokes for Jeremy. He enjoyed retelling Brian's jokes to Kerry's son, Jacob. Next, I did an online search for Kyle Peterson.

I was amazed when Kyle answered on the first ring. "I'm Peter Rogers, the recreation director for Whistling Pines. Brian Johnson suggested that I might be able to get a deal on a couple of dozen misshapen pumpkins to be used for senior citizen pumpkin painting."

"Sure, just come on out and collect a bunch of them. Nobody wants the lopsided ones that won't stand up. For that matter, any of them smaller than a bowling ball never sell either. You can have all of those that you want."

"That's fabulous! Where are you located?"

I wrote down the directions to Kyle's farm and thanked him. "Say, are you thinking about pumpkin bowling? That'd be a good use for them after you paint them."

"Wow. That's a great suggestion. I'll have to think about what we'd use as bowling pins. But if we've got the pumpkins, we'll find something to use as pins."

I posted the pumpkin painting notice on the bulletin board and walked to the director's office. Nancy looked up from her desk when I knocked on her door frame. "Hi, Peter. What's up?"

"I'm going to drive to a pumpkin farm later this week. Kyle Peterson offered free misshapen pumpkins for our pumpkin painting event."

"Wow, that's a creative approach to stretching your recreation budget."

"He also suggested pumpkin bowling. I think people would really get into that, but I need something to use as bowling pins."

Nancy's eyes brightened. "The grocery store did turkey bowling last Christmas. They used 2-liter pop bottles as pins. It was a hoot!"

"I think the grocery store has 2-liter bottles of generic soda pop on sale this week, two for a dollar. I'll pick up ten on my way through town."

I was about to leave when Nancy stopped me. "Has Kerry spoken to you about the fire at the bait shop?"

"He said it was arson."

"I think there may be an arsonist in town. This isn't the first business to have a fire."

"There's certainly an arsonist who set the bait shop fire, but I doubt there's a serial arsonist."

Nancy leaned back in her chair. "You and Kerry aren't from here. Tell Kerry to look back a couple of decades. I think he'll be surprised by the number of arson fires that have been set in failing local businesses."

Chapter 3

I was reading the *Duluth News Tribune* article about the bait shop fire when Jenny arrived at the table carrying a piece of toast and a mug of coffee.

"You're slipping, honey," she said as she sat down across from me.

"What?" I asked absently.

"You usually have coffee poured for me and bread in the toaster."

"I've been distracted by the news about the bait shop fire."

"Why would that distract you?"

"Nancy suggested that the fire might not be a one-time incident. I left a message for Kerry, suggesting that he check back through the department files on old fires."

"What did he say?"

"He didn't respond, which is unusual. He always calls back, even if it's just to needle me about something."

"I'm sure it's not personal. He's probably busy." When I didn't immediately respond, Jenny added, "Some people have a life."

"Uh-huh," I responded without registering Jenny's comment.

"Are you and Wendy going to play something during the costume contest?"

"Play something?"

"Peter, snap out of it. Are you planning to provide music during the Halloween costume contest?"

"I suppose the city band will play something."

"Earth calling Peter."

I looked up. "What?"

"You posted a notice for a Whistling Pines Halloween costume contest. Are you and Wendy going to play something during the judging?"

Trying to focus on Jenny's conversation after being engrossed in the story about the suspected arson at the bait shop, I set down the newspaper and took a deep breath. "I suppose we should do something."

"You sang 'Monster Mash' last year. Everyone sang along and enjoyed it. Maybe you could try something different this year."

After sounding like an elephant was coming down the stairs, Jeremy raced past us and grabbed a bowl, cereal, milk, and a spoon. "I need a Halloween costume," he announced as he poured milk over his cereal.

"Did you have something in mind?" Jenny asked.

"Can I borrow your pirate costume, Dad?"

"I think it's too big for you."

"I could roll up the sleeves and pants."

Discerning the real reason for the pirate costume, Jenny shook her head. "You aren't carrying a sharp sword around the neighborhood in the dark."

"Mom..."

"Not happening," Jenny replied. "What else sounds interesting?"

"Jacob is wearing his hockey uniform. I suppose I could wear my baseball shirt and carry a bat and glove."

"It's going to be cold. You'll have to wear the shirt over your jacket."

"Mom, that'll stretch it out."

The ringing of my cell phone interrupted the costume discussion. I stepped into the kitchen and accepted the call. "Can you be in my office ten minutes from now?"

"I have to wait at the bus stop with Jeremy. I could make it in half an hour."

"Okay. We'll be waiting in *your* office."

"We? Please tell me Meg won't be with you."

"Steve Zaccard is meeting me at the police station. We'll drive over."

"Who's Steve Zaccard?"

"He's the head Minnesota arson investigator."

"Why are you bringing him to my office?"

Kerry paused. "You left a voicemail for me yesterday. Or did you forget?"

"I thought you'd discounted it."

"Not at all. I called the state's arson investigation office and relayed your thoughts. Steve wants to follow up with you."

"Could we meet somewhere other than my office? It's sometimes…busy there."

"Peter, you just told me you didn't want to meet at the police station. Where else would you suggest?"

"How about the VFW?"

"I think it's a little early to start drinking for us Army people. I suppose you Navy guys say the sun is over the yardarm somewhere."

"They'll have a coffee pot on, and it'll be quiet there."

"I'll see you there in twenty minutes or so."

Jenny walked into the kitchen with a plate covered with crumbs in one hand and Amy on her opposite hip. "You're meeting Kerry at the VFW?"

"The state arson investigator wants to discuss Nancy's theory about a series of Two Harbors arson fires over the decades."

Jenny set her plate into the sink and ran water over it. "Please be careful."

"The VFW is pretty quiet."

"I'm more concerned about you and Kerry digging into old arson files than I am about the morning VFW clientele."

"What am I missing?" I asked.

"If there have really been decades of unsolved fires, there are people who don't want anyone digging into that history. There may be people who collected insurance payments on arson fires. You and Kerry digging into those cases could make waves that could lead to arrests."

"That's Kerry's problem."

Jenny sidled up to me and pecked my cheek. "You're so naïve."

* * *

In addition to Kerry and the fire chief was a man in a blue uniform with a small badge pinned to his shirt. They were seated at the table in the farthest corner of the empty VFW. "Steve, this is Peter Rogers, who suggested that our arson fire isn't an isolated event. Peter, this is Steve Zaccard, the captain of the Minnesota Arson Investigation Unit."

Steve, who was tall, stocky, and had a handlebar moustache that made me think he should be in a barbershop quartet, shook my hand and smiled. "Are you as colorful as Sparky?"

I shook my head. "No one is as colorful as our fire chief."

Sparky smiled, "I take great pride in bringing color to our town."

Grinning made Steve's moustache rise, somehow reminding me of the cartoon character Snidely Whiplash. "I saw the 'no newts' protest on the evening news."

Sparky's eyes sparkled. "I personally defused the protest."

"Sparky, I saw your interview on the Twin Cities evening news. But they were protesting newts, not nude models," Steve said.

"No one watching the news knew that, and I saved that young model's reputation."

I signaled Vern, the bartender, for coffee. "You didn't save her reputation, Sparky. She was the minister's daughter. All the protesters knew her and about her nude modeling for the art class."

Steve leaned forward. "I'm only a couple of years away from retirement. I'd like to get on the Whistling Pines waiting list if I could join your art class."

"They switched to male models after the protest," I replied.

Vern arrived with the coffee pot and topped off all the cups. He stared at Steve after filling his coffee cup. "Is there a barbershop quartet missing a singer?"

Steve tilted his head back and laughed. "I don't sing, but I do play tuba in the St. Paul Firehouse Band."

Oh Jeez, another tuba player, I thought to myself.

Kerry looked at me. "He's not quite as colorful as your friend Brian."

"I didn't say that out loud, did I?" I whispered to Kerry.

"You didn't have to say it. The thought was in all our minds."

Vern refocused the conversation on the art class. "Yeah, the Svenska Gotters ruined it for everyone. I was talking to Melissa about a veterans' art therapy class until Sparky chased off all the potential models."

Sparky sat up, looking offended. "I did NOT scare off the models. It was Peter's senior citizen painters who couldn't keep their mouths shut. Heck, they were posting the nude drawings in the Whistling Pines dining hall."

Kerry snorted his coffee. "I saw some of those drawings and I couldn't determine which were fruit and which were nudes."

"Kathy Christensen's drawings were..."

Kerry put up his hand to interrupt my defense of Kathy's quality drawings. "Can we move the discussion back to the fires?"

Vern rolled his eyes. "You know, Melissa was ready to instruct a class here, in the VFW. I think we could've packed this place."

"I'm not sure Melissa's male model would've drawn the crowd that Sherry Vogel would've attracted."

Vern shrugged. "I've been trying to come up with something that would bring in more female veterans. They need the camaraderie, too."

Steve watched Vern walk away, then pulled a sheaf of papers out of a leather portfolio. "At Kerry's suggestion, I did a database search on Two Harbors fires. There haven't been any more fires than I'd expect in a town of this size, but what's interesting are the number of small business fires that occurred when no employees were around and didn't result in a fatality."

I frowned. "Two Harbors has fewer arson fatalities?"

Steve ran his finger down a column of zeros. "There have been more than a dozen commercial fires in Two Harbors over the past thirty years, and none of them caused a fatality...until the bait shop fire. That's unusual unless there's an arsonist who waits until the building is empty. More than half of all commercial fires occur while there's someone in the building. Most people escape from the fire, but there are a percentage of fires that result in a fatality."

Pushing his coffee mug aside so he could get a better view of the pictures, Kerry said, "When I was investigating suspicious deaths in the Army, if there was a dead body inside a burned structure, the fire was usually set to cover up a murder."

Steve took out a sheaf of photos and spread them across the table. "Sparky's crew found a body under a collapsed wall in the basement last night."

Sparky pointed to white fragments among black ashes and charred wood. "The body was crushed, and the skeleton pulverized by the weight of the collapsed debris."

"I'm confused," I said, looking at the pictures. "Was the victim killed by the fire?"

Sparky let out a deep breath and shook his head. "We couldn't tell. It'll be up to the medical examiner to determine the cause of death."

"Have you identified the victim?" I asked.

Steve pointed to a burned wallet. "We haven't got a positive ID, but the leather wallet protected a driver's license and some charge cards that belonged to Elmer Antonich."

"Elmer Antonich, the retired hockey player?" I asked.

Sparky nodded. "Everyone called him 'Speedy' because he could skate faster backwards than forward. He was a Two Harbors hockey defenseman like none before or since."

Steve tapped his finger on the picture, refocusing our discussion. "The question is, why was Antonich in the bait shop when it burned? Was he the arsonist? Or was he an innocent victim?"

Kerry leaned back and drew a breath. "Was he the intended victim? Did the arsonist kill Antonich, then set the fire to cover up the murder?"

Steve gathered the pictures and put them back into his portfolio. "We'll have to wait for the medical examiner's report to know how Antonich died."

* * *

Although the Whistling Pines director had changed my duties to include acting as the public safety liaison, I always felt guilty meeting with Kerry away from the senior residence. I unlocked my office and hung my windbreaker behind the door. I'd barely opened my email when I felt a shift in the airflow.

"Why do cows wear bells?" Brian asked as he sat in my guest chair.

"What happened to your repertoire of tuba jokes?"

"Marybeth suggested I change up my joke inventory. Besides, you like jokes you can tell your son. Most of my remaining tuba jokes have adult themes. So, why do cows wear bells?"

"I think that joke is dated, Brian. Cows wore bells back when there were dairy herds. No one puts a bell on a beef cow."

Undeterred, Brian shrugged. "Back to the cows and bells. Why do they wear bells?"

"I don't know. Why do cows wear bells?"

Brian smiled, anticipating my reaction to the punchline. "Because their horns don't work."

I closed my eyes and groaned.

"Your son will love it!"

"I doubt that Jeremy will connect horns and cows. But I'll give it a try."

Brain leaned forward as I wrote down the joke. "I heard that Speedy Antonich committed suicide in the basement of the bait shop before he burned it down."

"Where did you hear that?" I asked as I placed the joke in my wallet.

"Steve Zaccard told me."

I clenched my eyes shut. "Why would the arson investigator tell you about an ongoing investigation?"

"He's part of the tuba brotherhood."

"You're kidding. There's a tuba brotherhood?"

Nodding emphatically, Brian said, "There aren't more than two dozen professional tuba players in all of Minnesota."

"You consider yourself a professional?"

"I get paid for my gigs with the polka band. That makes me a professional."

"Back to the arson investigation. Steve did NOT tell you that Antonich committed suicide. The cause of death hasn't been determined yet."

Brian slapped his thigh. "Ha! So, it was Speedy Antonich who died in the fire!"

I tilted my head back and stared at the ceiling. "Brian, I'd prefer that you not share that information until it's published."

"Too late!" he said, standing. "You just confirmed the rumor!"

"Please don't tell anyone."

"Who would I tell except Marybeth? Of course, she is playing bridge this afternoon and there are seven other women at the game."

"Don't..."

Without a reply, Brian disappeared.

Since my screensaver had already been displayed due to computer inactivity during the discussion with Brian, I left my email and walked to the dining room for a cup of coffee.

Bud Larson was having a discussion with Lee Westfall and Howard Johnson, his raised voice audible throughout the dining room. "Speedy played for the St. Louis Blues in the '60s. They won the Stanley Cup his second year with the team."

Howard, who always spoke with an indoor voice, shook his head. "He played for Montreal, and they never won a Stanley Cup during his years with them."

Bud frowned. "There's no way a kid from Two Harbors is going to play for a Canadian team. That would be treason! And I saw his championship rings."

Howard saw me drawing coffee from the urn and gave me a look of desperation. "Peter can look this up on his phone."

I sat in the empty fourth chair and looked at Lee, who'd moved to Two Harbors from Iowa. "What do you think, Lee?"

"I think this is one heck of a good argument. I'm enjoying it."

Bud pointed at my phone. "You look up Speedy Antonich and see what year he won that championship ring. I think it was '65."

It took a few seconds longer than usual to enter the search because Bud kept poking my arm, trying to make me go faster. "Easy, Bud. I make enough typos without your help."

"You spelled Antonich wrong. There's no V in it."

"I spelled it correctly, and here's his Wikipedia page."

Bud crowded close. "Yes, that's a picture of him when he was playing for St. Louis."

"Wikipedia says he played for Montreal from '61-'70. They won the Stanley Cup in '65, '66, '68, and '69. Antonich had four championship rings.

Bud shook his head emphatically. "Nope. That computer is wrong. He played with St. Louis."

I flipped to a different page. "St. Louis didn't get an NHL team until the 1967 expansion."

"That's B.S. I saw a game there when I was stationed at Fort Leonard Wood."

"What years were you in the Army, Bud?"

"I was drafted in...'68. Aw heck. Maybe it was Mike Sertich that I saw playing in St. Louis. He was from the Iron Range."

Bud stalked out of the dining room, leaving Lee and Howard smiling. Lee leaned back. "I love a good argument."

"Do you and Jeri argue?" Howard asked.

"Heck no. She'd have me cooking my own meals if I ever argued with her."

I chuckled.

"What's so funny?" Lee asked.

"You eat your meals here, in the dining room. Jeri doesn't cook for you."

"It makes no difference. The effect would be the same."

Howard leaned close. "Was it Speedy's body in the bait shop?"

"It appears that the cat is out of the bag," I replied.

Lee leaned forward and whispered, "There's a rumor that he shot himself, then started the fire."

Grimacing, I replied, "I think it'd be impossible for him to light the fire after he committed suicide."

"He probably didn't die right away. When people are shot, they don't just tip over dead like on TV. He could've shot himself and had lots of time to set the fire."

"Is there some reason to believe he'd shoot himself in the bait shop?" I asked.

"None at all," Howard replied. "I don't recall Speedy ever going fishing, so finding his body in the bait shop seems highly unlikely. Are they sure it was Speedy?"

"They found his driver's license with the body," I replied.

"So, they're convinced they have a positive ID?"

"Kerry mentioned something about dental records, but he's ninety-nine percent sure they've identified Antonich as the victim."

Chapter 4

Kerry knocked on the back door and walked in just as I was measuring coffee grounds into the coffee maker. He hung his cap and coat on hooks by the door and drew a breath. "I'd appreciate it if you'd make a couple of extra cups for me."

"You're here awfully early," I said as I covered the container and put it into the cupboard.

"I didn't get much sleep last night. Truth be told, I've been parked in your driveway for half an hour, waiting for the lights to come on."

"You *need* a cup of coffee."

Kerry sat in a kitchen chair and smiled. "I've already bought two cups of coffee from the gas station. I drank them while parked in your driveway."

"What's got you so riled up?"

"The arson fire and death. It's all so senseless. This morning's *Duluth News Tribune* headline is 'Local Hockey Legend Found Dead in Bait Shop Fire'. Our home phone rang constantly last night until I unplugged it at ten o'clock."

The coffee pot sputtered, signaling the end of the brewing cycle. I took three mugs down from the cupboard and filled two of them, handing the first one to Kerry and leaving an empty mug for Jenny. "Do you know anything new?"

Kerry clenched his eyes shut. "Not a thing. The medical examiner is performing the autopsy today. That may give us a cause of death and the identity of the victim."

Sitting across from Kerry, I sipped my too hot coffee. "Do you know any more about the cause of the fire?"

"An accelerant was used and there are multiple points of origin. It's obviously arson. But I don't have a clue about who lit the fire."

"You said an accelerant was used. Like gas?"

"I'm waiting for confirmation from the Minnesota arson investigator, but all indications are that the arsonist used gasoline to start the fire." Kerry paused. "And yes, I've already checked the security tapes at the local gas stations. No one filled four or five big gas containers in the past few days."

"Where does that leave you?"

"Well, he either bought the gas more than a couple of days ago or he bought a container of gas at four or five different stations. He might've bought that gas from a station farther outside of town. Or, he has access to a bulk gas tank on a farm."

"Are there fingerprints on the gas cans?"

"Gee, Sherlock. I wish I'd thought of that," Kerry said as Jenny walked into the kitchen wearing a bathrobe.

Jenny poured herself a mug of coffee as Kerry spoke. "What's the matter, Kerry? Isn't your sidekick providing critical insights that are solving your case?"

"I should probably lower my expectations." Kerry said with a smile. "Peter is just a civilian who throws out obvious thoughts."

"Hey!" I protested. "I didn't invite you in to insult me."

"I didn't insult you. I called you a civilian, which is what you are."

Shaking her head, Jenny asked, "Would either of you like a piece of toast or a bowl of cereal?"

Kerry stood. "Do you have a pair of travel mugs? Peter and I need to check out the victim's house."

Without hesitation, Jenny opened a cupboard and reached for the thermal travel mugs we'd acquired at an estate sale.

"I didn't agree to search the victim's house," I said, staying at the table. "I thought you'd have the Bureau of Criminal Apprehension handle your searches."

Kerry poured the remnants of his coffee mug into one of the travel mugs and topped it off from the pot. "They've got better things to do." He poured coffee into the second travel mug and screwed on the lid. "Come on. We should go before Jeremy comes down and our search becomes the talk of the school."

Smirking, Jenny bounced Amy on her hip. "I'll see you after work, Mr. Assistant Arson Investigator."

"Hang on. I have to work at Whistling Pines today," I protested.

Kerry put on his Two Harbors Police jacket and cap, then picked up the two travel mugs. "You know you want to be part of this investigation."

"I really don't, Kerry. I have a real job, with real responsibilities. I can't dash off to play cop with you whenever..."

"Don't make me call Nancy to request your assistance."

I stood and glared at Kerry. "That's evil. You know that she'll order me to help however I can."

"There's your answer," Kerry said, nudging the door open with the toe of his shoe. "Whatever I've got going on with this murder/arson investigation is more important than making popcorn for the afternoon movie."

Lifting my jacket off a hook, I pulled it on. "Just because my boss likes having me help you with investigations doesn't mean that I *want* to be involved."

Kerry winked at Jenny with his unscarred eye. "He loves it."

The front seat of Kerry's Two Harbors police car was crowded with a radio, computer, shotgun, and notepad. I squeezed into the passenger's seat and buckled the seatbelt.

"Do you ever use that shotgun?"

"It hasn't been out of the bracket since I took the job."

"Why keep it around up here. It's just more clutter. You could store it in the trunk."

Kerry backed onto the street. "Having been around Marines, you know how guns are. You don't need one until you need it badly and immediately."

I pondered that comment, thinking about how quiet Two Harbors was and how Kerry's shotgun seemed unnecessary. Then the reality of his words struck me. Every cop assumes his day is going to be quiet and boring. I'm sure it's that way right up until the unthinkable happens, and Kerry would be the one stepping into danger. A shotgun at his fingertips might be a difference between his life and death.

"What are we looking for at Antonich's house?"

Kerry shrugged. "We'll know when we see it."

"Is this a wild goose chase?"

"Not at all," Kerry replied. "This will give us a sense of who Antonich was. Knowing him better might help us understand why he was at the bait shop, and possibly, who was with him."

"It's October. Fishing season is over. I don't know why anyone would go to the bait shop."

"The store had been open during the day, so he must've had some business to justify staying open this time of year."

After a few moments of contemplation, I said, "Maybe it's a magnet for old guys who want to sit around and tell tales about fishing while they drink coffee."

Kerry glanced at me. "I knew there was a reason I wanted you along. That thought would never have crossed my mind."

"The men at Whistling Pines are always looking for an excuse to get out of the rooms and talk with the other guys. Some talk about cars, others just like to argue. Lee Westfall seems to stay uninvolved but likes to laugh when the others are arguing."

"I'll look through the pictures taken at the bait shop after the fire. Maybe there was a back room with a table, coffee pot, mugs, and chairs."

"I don't think they'd need a back room. I can picture guys sitting and standing around the display case while they argue about which bait is best for steelhead trout in October."

* * *

Elmer Antonich's house was only a few blocks away. Kerry parked on the street and took out a set of keys. "How did you get the keys?" I asked as we walked to the front door.

"They survived the fire in Antonich's pocket." Kerry tried two keys before he found the key that unlocked the front door. We were met with the odor of slightly old garbage and fried fish. Kerry stood inside the door, surveying the living room.

"What do you see?" I asked.

"There was a Mrs. Antonich at one time. She picked out the drapes and the furniture. Based on the magazines on the coffee table and the items in use, I'd say she's been out of the picture for quite a while."

"The recliner lined up in front of the television bears that out," I said. "If there was a second person living here, there would be a loveseat or two chairs with a view of the television." My eyes were drawn to a glass-fronted case across the room. "Look at the trophies, Kerry."

After handing me a pair of purple plastic gloves, Kerry pulled a pair onto his hands. We walked across the living room to the trophy case and knelt down. "Wow," Kerry said. "He's got high school and professional trophies and plaques in here. He was the Most Valuable Player in the 1966 Stanley Cup playoffs. Look at the picture of him holding the Stanley Cup."

"Kerry," I said, pointing to four huge, jeweled rings, each sitting on a clear plastic pedestal. "These are championship rings given to the players. They should be in a safety deposit box or somewhere more secure than a living room shelf."

"I suppose he liked seeing them and showing them off. They don't bring a lot of joy locked away in the bank."

"But they're worth thousands of dollars each. We can't leave them sitting here with no one to protect them."

"I'll ask a county judge to appoint a trustee to manage the estate. Maybe Meg Cochran would be willing to appraise the estate and secure the valuables."

"Meg might be over her head with the Stanley Cup rings. Isn't there an heir?"

Kerry shook his head. "I spoke with the neighbors. No one seems to recall Antonich having any visitors except the neighborhood kids. They loved him."

"Maybe he has a will in a drawer," I suggested.

"See if there's a desk somewhere with bank statements and financial papers. I'll check the kitchen and garage."

The house was small, with two bedrooms upstairs. One bedroom looked like I'd expect an old man's room to appear. The bed was unmade, and there were clothes hung on the backs of chairs and folded clothes piled on a dresser. It wasn't neat, but there weren't clothes strewn on the floor like we'd seen in the artist's studio during our investigation of the missing art professor.

The bathroom was utilitarian with an old-fashioned double razor, shaving cream, and aftershave set on top of the vanity along with a single toothbrush in a plastic cup and a tube of toothpaste. The medicine cabinet had a bottle of aspirin and a tube of hemorrhoid cream.

The second bedroom was an office. There were papers piled in neat and orderly stacks on top of the desk. I flipped through a pile of bills. Each was marked paid, in handwriting, along with the date and check number. The other pile contained deposit receipts, stock and investment papers, and bank statements. A quick glance at the investment information showed that Antonich opted to stay in his modest Two Harbors house by choice, not financial necessity. Alongside that pile sat a cracked vinyl checkbook cover. The check register notations were made in neat rows, with each row showing a new balance. The final balance was well over ten thousand dollars.

I opened the desk's lap drawer and found small containers of pens, pencils, paperclips, and push pins. A stapler and tape dispenser were in the back. A bulging white envelope caught my eye. Enclosed was a neat stack of one-hundred-dollar bills, all arranged so Benjamin Franklin was on the top and facing the same direction. I replaced the envelope in the drawer and made a mental note to tell Kerry.

I sat on the desk chair and opened a file drawer. The folders were neatly marked with tax years, then insurance policies, product warranties, and instructions for the appliances. The last file caught my eye. Social Security/Pension/Will.

I found a will dated July 1998. Quickly scanning it, I saw that Antonich had willed his estate to a niece and nephew, Penelope (Antonich) Peterson, and Karl Antonich. The will had been drafted by an unfamiliar lawyer, possibly someone who'd retired before my move to Two Harbors.

I put everything but the will back into the drawer and stood. Kerry startled me when he asked, "What did you find?"

"Antonich was more of an astute financial manager than most modern athletes. He's got a stock and bond portfolio that would allow him to own half the town if that's what he'd chosen to do, and an envelope with several thousand dollars worth of hundred-dollar bills."

Kerry looked into the hallway, then around the small office. "I wouldn't have guessed that based on his lifestyle. The fanciest thing he owns is a twenty-year-old Chevy pickup."

"There's a will giving the estate to a niece and nephew." I handed the will to Kerry. "I don't recognize the names, so I assume they live elsewhere."

Kerry nodded and lifted a gun case with his other hand. "I found a shotgun behind the kitchen door. He's probably owned this old double-barrel since he was a kid. I'll put it into the gun lockup in the police station. Let's put the championship rings into a container and count the cash. I'll secure them at the police station, too."

Kerry quickly counted out the cash as I watched over his shoulder. He made a notation, $5,700 on the envelope. "Sign the inner envelope by the amount and I'll put it in a sealed evidence bag."

"I suppose he kept the gun for protection."

Kerry looked around. "I don't think Antonich was concerned about being attacked or burgled. I found two ruffed grouse in the refrigerator. I think he kept the gun around for hunting. It's grouse and rabbit season."

"It *is* unloaded."

Kerry smiled. "Of course, it's unloaded. There's an orange coat on a peg with a handful of shotgun shells in the pocket. I suspect he'd grab his gun and coat, then drive out of town somewhere to shoot a grouse once in a while."

"Maybe he was in the bait shop asking about the best hotspots for grouse."

"Yeah," Kerry replied. "I guess we'll never know."

Kerry drove me to Whistling Pines in silence. "What are you thinking?"

I sighed. "I don't get it. Robbery wasn't the motive for killing Antonich. What happened?"

"I think he stumbled onto the arsonist and had to be eliminated as a witness."

"Why would he be at the bait shop late at night? It was closed."

Kerry pulled under the portico. "Who says he was there late at night?"

"The fire was in the middle of the night, long after the store closed. The owner was bowling his third game of the evening when they notified him."

"Antonich's body could've been in the basement all day. We'll have to see what the medical examiner says."

We sat idling in Kerry's car, staring at each other. I broke the silence, "I hate this. I was happier when I lived in my simple world with a wife and two children and was oblivious to the crime around me."

"The crime statistics say that if you stay out of the bars, don't use illegal drugs, lock your house and car, and don't pick any fights, your chances of being the victim of a crime are almost nil."

"Tell that to Elmer Antonich. I'm sure he'd be comforted by that knowledge."

Chapter 5

Putting the trip with Kerry out of my mind, I hung my coat in my office and walked to the dining room with my coffee cup. The late breakfast crowd was there, along with a few people who hung around to talk or play cards.

Karla Telker waved to me from the table where she was sitting with Kathy Christensen and Mary Gilbert. I drew a cup of coffee from the urn and sat in the fourth chair at their table. "Good morning, ladies."

Kathy leaned close. "We've decided on our Halloween costumes. I'm dressing up as Anne Shirley. Mary is going to be Diana Barry, and Karla is dressing as Marilla Cuthbert. We'll be dressed for tea."

I must've looked confused because Karla frowned. "You've never read *Anne of Green Gables*?"

"Sorry, that wasn't part of my high school bibliography."

Kathy put her hand on my arm. "It's wonderfully inspirational for young women. Anne Shirley is a redhead who's adopted by Marilla and Matthew Cuthbert."

I chuckled and looked at Karla. "You're going as Kathy's mother?"

"I'm not going to be Kathy's mother, per se. We'll be dressed as the adult versions of the characters."

"Do you already own those costumes, or are you going to make them?"

Mary's look told me their plan somehow involved me. "The Askov History Museum has closets filled with period dresses and suits. I spoke with Toni, the director, and she said we could rent them...if someone would drive us down to Askov. You don't have a field trip scheduled this afternoon and we thought a drive to the museum would be informative and fun."

"Why not," I replied, thinking a trip to the museum would be a nice way to distract myself from my thoughts about the arson scene and Elmer Antonich's house. "I'll post a sign-up sheet. You three can mention the trip to others."

Karla stopped me before I stood. "What did you read as a teenage boy?"

"I was a music nerd. I mostly played guitar and practiced with my saxophone for the band."

"You must've been assigned reading for English."

I drew a breath and thought back. "I read *Harry Potter* and *The Perks of Being a Wallflower*."

"I keep forgetting how young you are," she replied.

"Have you heard about anyone else's costume plans?" I asked as I stood.

Kathy sighed. "The men are duds. I don't think that any of them are planning to dress up at all."

"That's not true," Karla replied. "Kurt Hegland told me he's dressing as a sommelier. I guess he's got a dark suit and one of those wine tasting cups that he'll wear on a chain around his neck. He used to work for a wine distributor and hosted dozens of wine tasting events a year."

Responding to Mary's frown, I asked, "What's wrong?"

"I've never developed a taste for wine."

Kathy laughed. "Yes, Mary's church serves pre-fermented wine at communion."

"Pre-fermented wine?" I asked.

Mary nodded, "Grape juice. It's less controversial. Most of our congregation is anti-alcohol."

Hulda chose that moment to push her walker past. "Yeah, Mary's church is like the Svenska Gotters. They don't approve of anything that's fun: No drinking. No card playing. No gambling. No dancing."

I chuckled. "No posing in the nude for art classes, Mary?"

"I don't think that specific issue has come up before the deacons," she replied. "But I don't think they'd look favorably on it."

"See!" Huda said. "Nothing fun."

"We have women's circles and Bible study groups."

Hulda wrinkled her nose. "I suppose those would be okay if they served coffee and sweets."

Karla stepped in to redirect the conversation. "We all have our fellowship groups. Some of us meet with our friends at church. Others prefer venues like the bar. I've heard that Peter has a fellowship group with Pastor Olafson and some other veterans."

I froze as I considered Karla's characterization of our poker group in the pastor's office as men's fellowship. "Yes, it's a nice opportunity for those of us with battle scars to get together with others suffering from similar trauma."

Hulda, usually outspoken, and often confused, paused. "I suppose you vets with ESP need to get together and vent about shooting Nazis."

Karla, who'd taught in the same school, but after Hulda's retirement, cleared her throat. "ESP is Extra Sensory Perception. I think the vets suffer from PTSD, which is Post Traumatic Stress Disorder. And Nazis were long gone before any of today's vets served."

Hulda hated being corrected. She jerked her walker to the side, so she was aimed at the exit. "That's what I said. Peter and his Army friends have extra sensory stress disorder. I'm surprised any of them can hear or smell anymore." She toddled away.

Kathy had been suppressing laughter. "Gee, Peter, I didn't know you have a smell problem."

"Oh yes, my senses of smell, taste, rhythm, and humor have all disappeared."

Mary closed her eyes and clenched her fists together as if in prayer.

"Are you okay," Karla asked.

Mary glanced at Karla, then at me. "I'm praying that your senses come back again, Peter."

Smirking, I replied, "I hope so too. I'll really need my sense of rhythm before I sing during the costume competition."

Karla's eyes sparkled. "'Monster Mash'!"

"I'm trying to find a couple of new Halloween-themed songs to add to my repertoire."

"'The Ghostbusters Theme'," Mary suggested.

"'Witchy Woman', by the Eagles." Kathy suggested.

I put up my hand to stop the suggestions. "That's plenty. Thanks."

"One more, Peter," Karla said. "'Ding Dong the Witch is Dead'."

"That's good," I said, "but no more. I won't remember them all."

* * *

Ginny Johnson and Jeri Westfall were standing in front of the corkboard when I returned from my office with the sign-up sheet for the trip to Askov and the museum. Ginny, who has a bit of dementia, smiled. "I'm so looking forward to a museum trip. Where is it located?"

I mounted the sign-up sheet, which already included Mary, Kathy, and Karla. "It's in Askov. It's the Pine County History Museum, with displays of old Pine County photos, housewares, and a model train room."

Ginny stepped forward, and in shaky handwriting, added her name after Karla's. "I think that sounds like fun. Why haven't you taken us there before?"

Hesitant to point out that the van made a bi-monthly trip to the museum, and that Ginny had been with us at least a dozen times over the years, I just smiled. "It'll be a special treat for you, won't it?"

With a knowing smile, Jeri accepted the pen from Ginny and signed the sheet. "I hope we have time for a cup of coffee and a Danish in the Little Mermaid Café."

"I plan to be there for 90 minutes. You can manage your time however you like."

After signing her name, Jeri hung the pen in the holder alongside the cork board. "Karla said the firemen are making Booya for the Halloween festival."

"That's their plan. They're going to set up behind the bandstand."

Jeri sighed. "Lee loves Booya. I'm personally opposed to anything made with mystery meat and a secret recipe. If they won't share the recipe, I suspect there are unsavory components I don't want to eat."

Ginny got a dreamy look. "My husband loved Booya."

"How do you feel about it?" I asked.

She shuddered and made a smacking sound like she'd eaten something distasteful. "I'm not a fan of freezer-burned venison and overcooked vegetables."

"You're not the first person to share that opinion," I said, stepping aside so more people could sign-up for the museum trip.

Hulda Packer's walker rattled down the hallway toward us. I stepped aside to avoid the wheels that nearly ran over my toes. "I heard you're taking us out for lunch."

"No, I'm driving people to the Askov Museum."

Hulda pressed her nose close to the sign-up sheet. "Hmpf. This sheet is for the museum. Where's the restaurant sign-up sheet?"

"Some people are planning to have coffee and rolls at the Little Mermaid Café, located in the museum building. I'm not buying anyone lunch."

"That's false advertising. I was told you were buying us lunch."

"Who told you that?" I asked.

Cocking her head to think, Hulda was silent for a moment. "I think you told me."

"No. I haven't told anyone I'm doing anything but driving the van to Askov."

"I'll have to pay for my own lunch?"

"We're leaving after lunch is served in the dining room."

"I had my tastebuds set for Swedish meatballs and mashed potatoes with gravy."

"You can probably buy a plate of that at the Little Mermaid Café."

Hulda signed her name to the sheet. "I'll probably just have coffee and a Danish pastry."

To avoid further discussion, I returned to my office. I'd barely opened my email program when Wendy swept in. "I need your help."

"With what?"

"Our lead guitarist's fingers got smashed in a door while he was fighting with his girlfriend. I need you to fill in tonight at Hugo's."

"I think having a second child has ended my professional guitarist career."

Wendy sat in my guest chair and leaned her elbows on her knees. "How often have I asked you for a special favor?"

"About once a month."

"Well, this is a special Halloween dance. I really really need your help. Every other band is booked so there are literally no other guitar players available. Please, please, please."

"I'm going to be away from Jenny and the kids all day Saturday representing the Chamber of Commerce. I can't leave them tonight, too."

"I'll supply a babysitter so Jenny can come along. She likes listening to you play."

"Where are you going to find a trustworthy babysitter on short notice?"

Wendy stood. "Just tell Jenny that you're playing from 8-11 and that the babysitter will be provided...along with free drinks and food."

Wendy was halfway out of the door when I said, "I reserve the right to reject your babysitter if I think she's not trustworthy."

Wendy stuck her head in the door. "Deb Stone owes me."

"You're going to ask the police chief's wife to babysit my kids?"

"She's already told me she'll do it."

"You asked her to babysit before you even asked if I'd play?"

Wendy disappeared saying, "I knew you'd do it."

Chapter 6

Lunch was being served in the dining room when I walked past on the way to Jenny's office. I caught her in the hallway as she was locking the door. "Wendy asked me to play with her band tonight at Hugo's."

Jenny seemed unsurprised. "I know. We're getting free food and drinks, and Deb Stone is babysitting Jeremy and Amy at her house."

"Am I the last to know?"

Jenny reached up and touched my cheek. "Probably."

"Hey, I'm the one who's doing the work, but somehow my part seems irrelevant compared to the other logistics of babysitters and you joining me."

"I never get to hear you play and sing anymore. This is a treat."

"What if I'd said no?"

Jenny stepped into my personal space and smiled at me. "It's a date night. The kids are staying overnight at the Stones'. We'll be alone. All night. Without kids."

I must've smiled at the prospect of a romantic evening with my wife.

"How do you feel about having a third child?"

My mind had whiplash as it switched from romance to the topic of another child. "What?"

"Amy is almost a year old and men are less fertile once they hit forty."

"I'm not forty."

Jenny smiled. "What number do you get when you round off your age?"

"I feel like we've just gotten things under control. I think we shouldn't have more than one child at a time in diapers."

"How many spare hooks are under the fireplace mantel for Christmas stockings?"

"No. We aren't having enough children to use all those hooks. No way."

Jenny checked the hallway to make sure no one else was in sight. Then she unlocked her office, pulled me inside, and closed the door. She wrapped her arms around my neck. "We've talked about having another child."

"I'm not prepared to deal with two kids in diapers."

Jenny sighed. "Neither am I, right now."

I pressed my body against her. "You're a devil."

"When I need to be." She pushed me back. "Now, get back to work. There are probably people lined up for the van ride to Askov."

* * *

The drive to the museum took about ninety minutes. After unloading the seven people who'd signed up, I walked to the Little

Mermaid Café and sat at a table near the kitchen. I was eating a cheese Danish and sipping coffee when Kathy, Mary, and Karla walked in carrying long dresses. After draping them over a chair at a nearby table, they sat with me and ordered coffee and rolls.

"This place is a treasure," Kathy said. "Did you know that my grandmother's cookbooks and cast-iron cookware are displayed here?"

"I had no idea."

"My grandparents emigrated from Denmark and moved here when the Askov Lutheran Church still conducted services in Danish. Coming to this museum dredges up so many memories."

Mary laughed. "Like rutabaga festivals of yore."

"Rutabaga and potato sausage are comfort food," Kathy replied.

We talked about Askov's heritage and how the town had been a Danish version of Two Harbors with that city's Swedish and Norwegian roots. My group had all gathered in the café, so I stood, preparing to guide them to the van. Then, Hulda arrived.

"Is this where we get fed Swedish meatballs and mashed potatoes?" she asked as she pushed her walker into the dining room.

Thankfully, our waitress stepped out of the kitchen. "I'm sorry, but we sold out of meatballs at lunch and all the Danish are gone, too. We're shutting down the kitchen now."

Hulda snorted. "I came all this way, and I can't even get a meatball?"

I took her elbow and guided her toward the door. "We'll drive down for lunch on our next trip."

"Bah, I might not have a taste for Swedish meatballs then."

"I guess we'll have to wait and see," I replied as Mary and Karla laughed behind us.

"I think Hulda would eat Swedish meatballs if they were served with a side of sawdust," Karla whispered.

* * *

After dropping Jeremy and Amy off at Stones' house, Jenny and I drove to Hugo's. She was more antsy than usual. "Are you okay?"

"Do you know how long it's been since we had a date night?"

"Honey, it's not a date night. One of us is working," I reminded her.

"You'll love it. You always do. And I get to sip gin and tonic and listen to live music. We'll both be happy."

"I'm a little anxious. Wendy never gave me a setlist. I have no idea what we're playing."

"She said it's a Halloween-themed party. I suppose you'll be singing spooky songs."

"That's a long song list with a lot of variety. It could be everything from "The Skeleton in the Closet" by Louis Armstrong to "Haunted" by Taylor Swift."

"What's the problem? You know them all."

"I haven't practiced or played many of them in years."

Jenny reached out and squeezed my hand. "You'll do fine. You always do."

Hugo's gravel parking lot was nearly full when we arrived. I found a spot blocking the dumpster and retrieved my guitar from the trunk. "I hope there's a place for you to sit."

"Trust me. There's always an empty chair for the lead guitar player's girlfriend."

"Um, you're the guitar player's wife, not his girlfriend."

Jenny laughed. "What's the matter, are you afraid someone's going to pick me up?"

"The last time I played here, someone hit on *me*."

Jenny took my hand as we walked inside to loud voices and the smell of beer and sweat. "I can guarantee that we'll be going home together."

Wendy waved at me wildly from the tiny bandstand. Then she pointed to an open seat at a table in the front and mouthed, "Jenny."

I pulled Jenny along through the rowdy crowd until we broke through next to the bandstand. The empty chair was at a table where Nancy, the Whistling Pines director, and her husband, Brandon were seated.

They stood and hugged Jenny. Brandon held the empty chair out for her. "We had orders to save a chair for the guitarist's wife," he said with a smile.

Wendy stowed my guitar case while I tuned, then re-introduced myself to the band.

Wendy sat on a stool and turned on the mic. "Hi, folks. For those of you who don't know us, we're the Gin Fizzes. We have a special guest tonight. Peter Rogers is playing lead guitar." After a round of applause, Wendy went on. "In honor of Halloween, we're playing a set of seasonal music. You may remember this 60s hit from The Classics IV." I played the opening guitar riff from "Spooky", and Wendy joined in, singing the lyrics made famous by Dennis Yost, the Classics IV lead singer.

Scanning the crowd, I noticed Sparky at a table in the second row with a group of young firemen. He was getting into the music, and I caught a few looks between Wendy and him that seemed like more than casual eye contact with the crowd. Wendy stepped down from the stage as she started the third verse, flirtatiously touching a few guys on the shoulder until she got to Sparky.

Without returning to the stage, Wendy sang the opening of "Unchained Melody." As she touched her fingertips to his face, Sparky slid his chair away from the table and Wendy sat on his lap. The crowd laughed, assuming he was just a random guy she was flirting with. I could see the look on their faces. When the second verse ended, Wendy kissed Sparky, lingering so long that I started singing the third verse solo. Wendy joined in halfway through the verse and we continued the duet until she stepped onto the stage as the song ended.

I put my hand over the microphone. "What the hell, Wendy."

"He's cute. I think we had a moment."

"A moment? It looked like you were doing a lap dance."

After a couple of oldies, Wendy reached for a water bottle and announced, "It's time to move ahead a few decades. "This is 'Haunted' by Taylor Swift." The change threw me. and I struggled through a few bars until I remembered the complicated chord sequence.

After we played "Thriller" and "The Ghostbusters Theme", Wendy took another drink from her bottle. "All right folks, are you ready for something that's going to challenge our fill-in guitar player?"

The crowd cheered as Wendy gave me a mischievous look. "What?" I asked, my words lost in the crowd noise.

"Let's see if Peter can channel Carlos Santana." Wendy's grin was devilish as I shook my head. "Let's play 'Black Magic Woman'," she said.

Aside from having some of the most challenging guitar solos in any pop song, I hadn't played the music in a couple of years. "Wendy, no."

The drummer started the beat, and the bass guitar played the opening bass line. I tipped my head down, closed my eyes, and tried to let muscle memory play the opening guitar riff. Shutting out the crowd, I focused on Carlos Santana's famous and challenging notes that opened the song. Wendy sang the opening lyrics.

I took a breath, having hit every note. When the song ended, I was physically and emotionally drained. I looked at Jenny, who was standing and cheering with everyone else in the bar. Tears were streaming down her face, and I could almost feel her bursting with pride.

During the break between sets, Nancy handed me a beer. Leaning close to be heard over the rowdy crowd, she said, "You looked panicked when Wendy announced, 'Black Magic Woman'."

"I haven't played it in years."

"You didn't miss a note."

I took a swallow of beer. "I'm not sure how."

"You have an amazing ability to become one with your instrument. You don't play it, you make music. It's truly your gift."

"Yeah, I wish Wendy would give me the playlist a day or two before the gig."

"Part of the show is your look of shock when she introduces the songs."

"I'm not faking that look."

Nancy laughed. "The crowd doesn't know that."

After the break, we transitioned to familiar songs including "Monster Mash". Looking at the clock, I realized we'd been onstage for three hours. I assumed we'd played the last song when the crowd started chanting for an encore.

Wendy took the mic and looked at me. "How's your falsetto, Peter?"

I shook my head. "I haven't sung this much in months. I think my falsetto exited the room."

Wendy said something to the bass player and drummer. "This song was originally done by Maurice Williams and the Zodiacs. Most of you might remember the cover done by Jackson Browne."

Wendy sang the opening stanza, "Oh won't you stay…just a little bit longer." And I joined in on the chorus. The last verse usually included a falsetto. Wendy's alto voice couldn't hit the notes and my falsetto had been strained earlier. I played the notes on the guitar, then sang the falsetto, "Oh won't you stay…". The bar went wild. We wrapped up the song. Dozens of people came forward to slap our backs and stuff cash into the fishbowl Wendy set on the edge of the bandstand.

With my guitar packed up, Nancy and Jenny edged close to me. Nancy pecked my cheek. "My brush with stardom."

I snorted. "Hardly."

I'd picked up my guitar case and turned to leave when a blonde pushed herself against me. She reached behind me and squeezed my butt before whispering something I couldn't hear over the crowd. I was trying to take a backward step when Jenny pushed herself between the blonde and me. "He's mine."

The blonde, drunk and disoriented, didn't understand. Jenny was nose to nose with the inebriated woman. "Really, honey. The lead guitar player is mine. We're leaving together."

We slid away, with Nancy's husband inserting himself between the pouting woman and the door. Jenny had my hand and we nearly jogged across the parking lot, dodging cars that were pulling out and people who wanted to talk to me.

Inside the car, she leaned over and put her head on my shoulder. "I'm so proud of you."

"I'm a little rattled."

I felt her hand on the inside of my thigh. "Take me to your bedroom, Mr. Rockstar. I feel like a groupie tonight."

I laughed. "You're so bad at that."

"Really? You don't think that I'll be able to fill your every desire?" She kissed me, then looked into my eyes. "Seriously, take me home. I want to make love to my rock star husband."

She hummed "Stay". As I turned onto the road, I noticed Wendy standing next to a pickup with her arms draped around Sparky's neck. I nodded toward them. "Speaking of groupies..."

"Who is the guy with her?"

"That's Sparky, the fire chief."

Looking over her shoulder, Jenny said, "I always thought he was older."

"Kerry said none of the other firemen wanted the job, so they chose Sparky."

Chapter 7

I was drawing coffee from the dining room urn when a gruff voice called my name from across the room. Darrell Sanders was waving at me from a table near the windows. I was surprised that Darrell, a fairly new addition to the residence, was beckoning me to his table. I assumed he had a question about the recreation programs. "What can I do for you, Darrell?"

"Lee Westfall told me you help the police chief with investigations. Are you looking into the arson fires?"

"I don't really help the police chief. Our sons are friends, and he sometimes bounces ideas off me."

"Let me bounce an idea off you. I've lived in Two Harbors my entire life and was a volunteer fireman for decades. The fire at the bait shop was different from the others."

"Different how?"

"First of all, Speedy Antonich died in the fire. The arsonist in the past made sure no one was in the buildings that burned. Secondly, the bait shop wasn't in financial trouble. It's the only place to buy bait between Duluth and Silver Bay. They do a booming business all summer and most of the winter. The police were suspicious of the old arson fires because all the businesses that burned were on the verge of bankruptcy."

"You're saying the other business fires were arson, too?"

Darrell shrugged. "It's a poorly kept secret that nearly every failing Two Harbors business has burned down for the past hundred years."

"The police reports are ambiguous."

Darrell made a scoffing sound. "The police never identified an arsonist, and the owners always had ironclad alibis, so no arrests were ever made. That doesn't mean there wasn't a connection between the owners' financial situation and the convenient timing of the fires. The businessmen, the banks who held the mortgages, and the community all benefited from those fires. Do you think anyone looked too closely at them?"

"The police must've investigated them."

"I'm sure they did a diligent job of investigation. But face it, only dumb and unlucky criminals are caught. Whoever lit those old fires was smart. They weren't lit by some kid who dumped a can of gas on the floor and lit a match. I was at those fires and the point of ignition wasn't ever obvious. There was a lot of discussion around the firehouse and the consensus was that the arsonist used timing devices, so he was far from the scenes before the full conflagration occurred."

"You mean, like the timer on a bomb?"

"There are a hundred ways to light a wick that won't burn until minutes or hours later."

I frowned. "You've obviously thought about this. Give me an example."

"A lit cigarette continues to burn for several minutes. If someone were to insert something flammable into it near the filter, the fire wouldn't ignite until several minutes after the arsonist was gone. Hell, a drop or two of lighter fluid in the cigarette filter will flame when the tobacco burns down to the end."

"Okay, that'll give the arsonist a couple of minutes to escape. Is that a particularly smart way to delay the fire?"

"Sure, it is! All the evidence burns up in the fire. All you've got is ashes that get washed away in the water."

"Are there other delayed ignition sources like that?"

Darrell leaned close. "Peter, there are hundreds of them. I'm sure anyone smart like you could find a couple of dozen techniques in a two-minute internet search."

I considered that comment for a second. "You're convinced the bait shop arson was different."

"I heard the arsonist dumped cans of gas on the floor. That's risky and causes an immediate conflagration. Gas fumes ignite fast, and an inexperienced arsonist is often burned by the gasoline flash."

"Gas fumes?"

"Liquid gas doesn't burn. It has to evaporate into fumes to ignite. Once the fumes ignite, they heat the remaining liquid and it burns fast. If you let gas evaporate too long, or if the environment where the gas is spilled is too warm, in an enclosed space, you get an explosion. Boom!"

Darrell seemed to be done, so I stood and took my coffee cup. "Thanks for the arson lesson."

"Just tell the chief that this new arsonist is a different person from the one who lit the old fires."

"I imagine so. Some of those fires date back to the 1960s. Whoever lit them is old now, or dead."

Darrell chuckled. "He's probably living here."

Reflecting on the conversation as I walked away, I thought back to Darrell's last words, *He's probably living here.*

I entered my computer password and pulled up Google. After typing in *arson,* I looked at the pages of reported arson fires. There seemed to be about a hundred news articles every day about arson fires. Narrowing the search to *how to start an arson fire* yielded a different set of results, but with just as many articles and a selection of YouTube videos. Watching a video on my computer of a fireman starting a fire with a block of peroxide, I sensed someone behind me.

"Are you planning a new career as an arsonist, Doc?" Brian Johnson asked.

Clicking my mouse while attempting to turn off the video, I instead started George Strait singing "Amarillo by Morning".

Laughing, Brian sat in my guest chair. "Guilty conscience?"

Instead of turning off the video, I turned. "I had an interesting conversation with Darrell Sanders about arson. He suggested that anyone could learn how to set a fire from the internet."

"Well, you can watch a YouTube video about how to play a tuba, but that doesn't prepare you for a gig with a polka band."

"True, but some of the stuff is pretty basic."

"A kid with a can of gas and a match can start a fire. I think being a true arsonist takes more finesse."

"Darrell mentioned techniques for delayed ignition. An arsonist could be minutes or hours away from the site before the fire ignites."

Brian leaned back and crossed his legs. "Beyond that, I think whoever set some of the blazes around town used techniques that left the origin of the fire in question. I don't think the investigators could ever point to specific evidence indicating the fire was arson versus an accidental event."

"Like a grease fire in a restaurant," I suggested.

Brian nodded. "Or the lumberyard fire that seemed to have started in a pile of sawdust. It might've been ignited by someone's discarded cigarette, or it may have been sparked by a steel saw that hit a rock chip. All they ever knew was that it started near the saw and nearby sawdust pile."

"Do you know if insurance paid for the fire damage in all those fires?"

Brian shrugged. "None of the businesses ever rebuilt, but I don't know if they didn't receive enough to rebuild, if the owners decided to retire, or if there wasn't an insurance payout." After a pause, he added, "The best source of that information probably lives here. Miranda Paulson was secretary for her husband's insurance agency. If they didn't insure the buildings, I'm sure she and her husband, Jerry, knew the agents who issued the coverage."

My smile must've confused Brian.

"What?"

"That's possibly the most useful piece of information you've ever provided to me."

Standing, Brian shook his head. "Don't get accustomed to it. If word gets out that I've been helpful, people will expect it of me and that's really against the tubists' code of conduct."

"Tuba players have a code of conduct?"

"It's informal. We generally aspire to be less than helpful. It keeps people's expectations low, so we don't disappoint them." With a cherubic grin, he paused at my door. "You do know the secret to happiness, right?"

"I'm sure you're about to tell me."

"Keep your expectations low."

Chuckling, I replied, "I think there's a quote from Tony Hillerman, a guy who writes mysteries set in the Southwest. 'Don't expect much from life and you'll be seldom disappointed.'"

"I like that. Was he a tuba player?"

"I doubt it."

"Too bad. He sounds like my kind of guy."

I shut down my computer and decided to look for Miranda Paulson. The residents were gathering for the weekly movie, where I found Miranda sitting next to Ginny Johnson. I plopped down next to her, interrupting their discussion. "Excuse me, but I was wondering if you could answer an insurance question for me."

Miranda smiled. "I'm afraid I've been retired for too long to have any current information, Peter."

"I'm actually looking for something more historical. Do you know if the owners collected insurance after their businesses burned down in the '60s and '70s arson fires?"

"I'm sure they did. None of the owners were complicit in the arson, so they collected on their policies."

"There were investigations that showed that the owners weren't involved?"

"Certainly! The police, fire marshal, and insurance investigators all checked out the fire scenes and interviewed the owners. They all concluded that someone torched the buildings, but it wasn't the owners."

"Were the owners suspects?"

"I'm sure they were, but all of them had alibis for the time of the fire, so the investigations cleared them all."

"Why are you asking? Is there some suspicion about the bait shop fire?"

"Not that I know about," I replied as the lights dimmed for the movie.

Chapter 8

Being the first adult home from work meant I was responsible for preparing dinner. Lacking inspiration, I opened the freezer and found a pan of frozen lasagna. I resisted my natural instinct to throw it into the oven at 350° until it smelled done and flipped the package over. I read the instructions and set the oven timer for the suggested 45-50 minutes.

I found Jeremy in the dining room hunched over a pile of homework. To his side sat a plate with the remnants of a peanut butter sandwich and an empty glass. "Do you have any questions?" I asked, thinking about his homework.

"When are we eating?"

"The lasagna will be done in 45 minutes."

Jeremy looked up. "That's like almost an hour."

"Yes, it's three-quarters of an hour."

Giving me what was becoming a tiresome look of disdain, he replied, "Can't you cook it faster? I'm hungry now."

"Your mother isn't home yet, so even if it was ready now, we wouldn't be eating immediately."

"But I'm hungry."

"It appears you ate a sandwich and drank a glass of milk."

Refocusing on his math worksheet, Jeremy shook his head. "That was like hours ago."

Not wanting to point out that he'd only been home from school for half an hour, I walked upstairs to change into jeans and a t-shirt. I heard the television as I walked downstairs. Jeremy was eating a Pop-Tart, crumbs covering the couch cushion.

"Are you through with your homework?" I asked, hoping to be heard over the sounds of the nature show he was watching.

"Yeah."

"All of it?"

"Except for the English paper. It's not due until tomorrow. I can finish it in class."

"If you did it now, you wouldn't have to rush through it tomorrow before class."

"Dad, they give us time to write in class."

"But if you did it now, I could correct the spelling and punctuation."

"That's what the teacher does when she corrects it."

Letting out a sigh, I said, "Let's do it now and you can correct it and get a better grade."

"Mrs. Christen doesn't care about the spelling. She grades us on our creativity."

"I'm sure you're getting extra credit for your creative spelling."

Not *getting* the sarcasm, Jeremy ignored me.

Stepping outside the back door, I dialed Kerry's cell phone. I noticed a pickup and trailer backed up to the rental house next door. If not for what I knew about the sorry state of the young neighbors' belongings, I might've suspected they were being robbed. I saw two shaggy young men arguing as they carried a moth-eaten sofa from the house.

"What's up?" Kerry asked.

"Brian Johnson stopped by my office today and actually offered a useful suggestion. He said Miranda Paulson and her husband had owned an insurance agency. Miranda told me the insurance companies paid for the fire damage from the arson fires in the '60s and '70s. The investigations showed that the fires were arson, but the owners all had alibis for the time of the fires."

"I guess that doesn't surprise me. That doesn't mean that the owners weren't involved, but it shows that they didn't light the fires themselves."

"I also spoke with Darrell Sanders, who used to be a volunteer fireman. He suggested that the new bait shop fire was the work of a different arsonist. He felt that the historical fires were lit by someone with more finesse. The bait shop fire was created by slopping gas on the floor and then lit. He said the older fires had obscure ignition sources that made it hard to determine exactly how the fire had been set."

"Those are interesting insights I didn't pick up from the old files," Kerry said before pausing to think. "It's interesting that an old fireman brought these observations to you. I wouldn't expect someone like him to be that insightful."

"I imagine firemen are like soldiers, sailors, and Marines. There are long periods of boredom where lots of the world's problems are discussed and solutions proposed."

Kerry laughed. "If only Congress had listened to us. The world would be a better place."

"So, what are you going to do with Darrell's insights?"

"They're filed away in my safe-like brain. I'll have to think about his observation that the bait shop fire was ignited very differently from the others. Your source makes it sound like the same person lit all the fires way back when."

"Yes, someone canny in the use of delayed ignition sources and different kindling materials."

"Most criminals find something that works and stick with it. I'm sure the investigators thought they were seeing the work of several different arsonists if the fires were set differently."

"I'm not sure that those fires weren't the work of different people. Darrell may have been telling me about his observations about the complicated delayed ignition devices used in those historic arson fires."

"That's a whole different approach than dumping gas and lighting it."

"On the other hand, whoever lit those old fires is either very old or dead. It's not surprising that a different arsonist would use an alternate ignition source.”

“It’s more than that, Peter. The older fires were set by someone who was educated and careful. The bait shop arsonist is probably lucky that he didn’t light himself on fire when the gas ignited.”

“Have you checked the local clinics and hospitals for burn victims?” Peter asked.

“Gee, why didn’t I think of that?” Kerry said. “I’ve spoken to every clinic and the lead ER doctor in every hospital from Duluth to the Canadian border. No one has treated a burn victim with injuries consistent with a gas conflagration.”

“Maybe he’s hiding at home until his eyebrows grow back.”

“Great observation! Why don’t you go door-to-door pretending to be collecting signatures on a petition. While you’re at it, you can check everyone’s eyebrows.”

“I think that’s beyond my vague responsibility as the public safety liaison.”

“I think that falls under the heading, ‘other duties as assigned.’”

I was going to argue, but Kerry hung up before I replied.

Seeing more people carrying furniture out of the neighboring house, I decided to walk over and see who was moving out and if they knew who our new neighbors were. Before I could step inside the open front door, Rambo, the large friendly dog, stuck his nose into my crotch. "Um, hi, Rambo. Nice dog. Don't bite me."

Although Rambo looked scary, he was friendly. The most damage he'd done to me was leaving slobber on my pants.

"Hey, Peter," our neighbor, Tim said, as he set a box into the trailer.

"You're moving?" I asked as he set the box on top of the sofa they'd carried out earlier.

Tim stopped next to me, as a young man I didn't recognize, set down a lamp in the pickup bed. "The band broke up. I couldn't afford the rent without roommates to pay a share."

I looked into the house. "How's Zoey handling the band break up?"

"Actually, it was Zoey who broke up the band. She's moved on."

"Ah," I replied. "It's hard to have a band without a lead singer. Were you having creative differences?"

Tim shrugged as his friends carried out other boxes and garbage bags full of clothing. "It wasn't so much creative differences as it was her getting all uptight about our lives."

"I don't understand."

Tim shrugged. "You're a guitar player, so you understand how there are always groupies hanging around who are willing to get it on with you. Zoey thought we were exclusive. I was taking advantage of the 'flavor of the day.'"

"And Zoey objected to you sampling the flavor of the day."

Tim cocked his head. "How does *your* wife deal with that when you play a gig?"

I laughed. "Jenny's made it clear to a few women that she's the one going home with the guitar player."

Tim frowned. "You're okay with that?"

"I never got into the groupie thing. Drunk women put me off."

A guy with a few days' beard growth stopped and glared at Tim. "Listen, man. If you're not carrying your own shit out of the house, I'm out of here."

Tim nodded and walked inside.

"Do you know who the new renters are?" I asked as he walked away.

"No clue," he yelled over his shoulder.

I walked back home, thinking about Zoey being unhappy with Tim's interest in other women. Hearing the timer buzzing when I walked into the kitchen, I rushed to the oven and took the lasagna out.

Jeremy was setting the table as Jenny walked in with Amy in her arms. She watched me peel off the aluminum foil that covered the lasagna pan. "That smells wonderful. Do we have any Italian dressing for the salad?"

I grimaced, having lost thought of side dishes during my discussion with Tim. "No salad," I replied. "I saw the neighbors were moving and I got distracted when I talked to them."

"I saw the pickup and trailer. Do we know who is moving in?"

"Tim didn't know if the owner had a new renter."

Jenny took Amy out of her carrier and unzipped her jumper. "Tim and Zoey seemed nice. They were good neighbors when they stopped practicing music all night."

I found a serving spoon in the drawer and set it next to the lasagna pan. "Apparently, Zoey took a dim view of Tim's interest in groupies."

Jeremy stuck his head around the corner. "Are groupies a kind of fish?"

I grimaced and Jenny rolled her eyes. She waited to see how I would answer the question. "Bands are sometimes called groups. Some groups have dedicated fans who go to all their performances. Those fans are sometimes called groupies."

"Why was Zoey mad at Tim about their fans?"

I waited for Jenny to reply. When she didn't, I said, "I think he was spending too much time talking to the fans and not paying enough attention to Zoey."

Grinning, Jenny hung her jacket on a peg by the door and changed the topic. "You know there isn't any fiber in a serving of lasagna. I'd like a salad, too. Do we have any lettuce?"

"There's no lettuce. It's okay. I'm sure we're all regular enough. Skipping one portion of fiber won't cause a bowel impaction."

Jenny shook her head. "You are so clueless."

"Yup, that's me, clueless Peter. What would you like to drink with your lasagna?"

"I think we'll all drink milk."

"So much for dad's beer," I grumbled.

"What did Kerry have to say?" Jenny asked as she strapped Amy into her highchair.

"I had a discussion with Darrell Sanders about arson. I hadn't known that he'd been a volunteer fireman."

"I only remember him as the very knowledgeable go-to guy at the hardware store. I could bring in anything and he'd find a replacement part and explain how to make the repair."

"We had an interesting discussion about setting fires."

Jeremy perked up when he heard that news. "Like what?"

Jenny's headshake was unnecessary. A year of fatherhood had taught me tough lessons about off-limit topics that Jeremy found way too interesting. "Most arsonists use a match," I said, hoping that was the end of the discussion.

"Is that how the guy lit the bait shop on fire?" he asked.

"Probably," Jenny quickly replied. "Are you through with your homework?"

"Mom, I always do it when I get home from school."

"Yes, you're very good about that, but you sometimes run out of time before you get *all* your homework done."

"I did everything except my English paper. I'll finish it in class."

The homework discussion was interrupted by a knock on the back door. I set my silverware aside and stood up as Jeremy peeked past me to see who had arrived.

The fire chief was standing on the step looking uneasy. "Hi, Sparky. What can I do for you?"

"Gosh, it looks like I've interrupted your dinner. I'm sorry. I'll catch you another time."

"Have you eaten yet?" I asked.

"I'm going to grab a bite in town."

I opened the door and stepped back. "Come in, we've got a huge pan of lasagna."

"I hate to intrude."

"Come in, Sparky. We've got plenty extra."

I took his coat and led our visitor into the dining room. "Have a seat here. Jeremy, please get a plate and fork for the fire chief."

Seeing Sparky's uniform brought Jeremy to life. He jumped up and raced to the kitchen as Sparky nodded to Jenny. "Hi, Mrs. Rogers. I'm sorry to interrupt..."

Jenny wiped Amy's mouth as she bounced, happy to see someone new at the dinner table. "Please join us, chief."

I dished a large portion of lasagna onto Sparky's plate as Jeremy poured another glass of milk. "Is this a social call, or did you have something special on your mind?"

After putting a forkful of food in his mouth, Sparky looked at Jenny. "Actually, I need some girlfriend advice."

Jenny raised her eyebrows. "From me?"

Sparky nodded. "You know Wendy, and well, I'm kind of falling for her."

Jenny grinned and looked at me. "I don't know what I can tell you."

"I haven't dated a lot and Wendy is..." To his credit, Sparky looked at Jeremy and considered his words. "She's offering encouragement that I'm unaccustomed to. I'm not sure that I'm reading the signals correctly."

Jenny raised one finger to pause Sparky. "Jeremy, if you're through with your lasagna you can put your plate in the sink and start working on your English report in your room."

"But Mom..."

"Your dad and I want to have a discussion with the chief. Please work on your paper, okay?"

Jeremy left unhappily, leaving Sparky looking uneasy. "I'm sorry. I didn't mean to disrupt your evening."

Jenny waved off Sparky's apology. "It's fine. Jeremy needs to start that paper."

Having never really engaged Sparky in conversation before, I studied him as he ate. He was close to my age, younger than I'd thought. I remember him handling the news people during the art studio protest with humorous aplomb. Talking about Wendy was an uncomfortable topic. He stared at Amy, who was happily smearing lasagna around the tray of her highchair as if she was fingerpainting.

"Is it okay to talk with the baby here?" he asked.

Jenny smiled at Sparky's lack of child knowledge. "Amy won't understand a word that you say."

Sparky paused, trying to compose his thoughts. "I haven't dated for a couple of years and, well, Wendy is more forward than the girls I dated back then. I'm not sure how to take her."

Jenny looked at me with a pained expression, signalling her reluctance to talk about Wendy. I swallowed my last bite of lasagna and realized that Sparky had cleaned his plate. "Would you like another serving?" I asked, delaying my inevitable responsibility for answering his question.

"That'd be great!" he replied, sliding his plate closer to the lasagna pan.

"Wendy doesn't hold much back," I replied as I scooped up another portion of lasagna and slid it onto Sparky's plate. "She's comfortable in her own skin and she speaks her mind."

"I get that," Sparky replied. "I'm cool with someone who shares what she thinks. It's more the physical aspect of our dates that confuses me."

I set my fork on my plate and leaned back. "As Wendy's co-worker, I'm not sure I should engage in a conversation about your joint sexual experiences."

Sparky shook his head. "Don't get me wrong. There hasn't been any sex. That may be the direction we're going, but I'm not sure how to read her...signals. The last time I dated, the guys were trying to get the girls into bed and the girls were determined not to let that happen. It was kind of a mating dance that never led to anything but 'stop.'"

Jenny grinned. "And Wendy hasn't said stop, so you're not sure what's going on?"

Sparky nodded. "That sums it up pretty well. You probably saw us at Hugo's. I got to second base in the parking lot."

I glanced at Jenny and mouthed, *second base?*

She smiled and glanced at her chest.

"That was a problem?" I asked.

"Well, yes. It's not like we could take another step standing there with twenty people walking to their cars. And I couldn't invite her back to my place. I live with my mother. And my pickup doesn't have a back seat."

I looked at Jenny, who signaled she wasn't going to join the conversation but was happy to watch me squirm. "I'm not sure what to tell you, Sparky. Maybe you should make a plan for your next date that includes a motel room."

"That's part of my problem. I haven't asked her out since Hugo's. It's been a couple of days and I'm feeling kind of embarrassed because I haven't called her. And the reason I haven't called is because I don't know what to say."

Jenny finally jumped in with a female perspective. "Call her as soon as you leave. Apologize for not calling her earlier and explain to her that you've been tied up with the arson investigation. Pick a nice restaurant and take her out for dinner. Then, see where things go."

"What if I'm getting signals that she's not really interested in...whatever."

"You kiss her cheek when you take her home and you move on."

Sparky shook his head. "I'm so out of touch with reading signals. I don't want to cross a boundary."

Chuckling, I smiled. "Wendy doesn't mince words. You'll know exactly where she stands. If she's not interested in anything past supper, she'll let you know. If you're approaching one of her boundaries, she'll tell you to stop."

Stirring his last bite of lasagna in the sauce, Sparky stared at his plate. "It's been a couple of years since..." He continued to stir the lasagna and Jenny and I awaited his question. "Have there been any changes in women's underwear I should be prepared for? I mean, I don't want to seem like a total loser if we get to a point where I'm supposed to know how something works but I really don't."

Unable to contain her laugh, Jenny snorted. "Trust me, Sparky, if Wendy wants something removed, she'll either take care of it or she'll guide you through the process."

Sparky popped the last bite of food into his mouth as he nodded. "Thanks for supper and the advice."

Jeremy raced down the stairs and walked into the dining room. "Are you through with your grown-up discussion? I have a question about my English paper. Mrs. Christen said she wanted two pages. Does that mean two pages full of words, or does that mean enough words so I have to start a second page?"

Surprising both Jenny and me, Sparky answered, "My teachers always meant two whole pages. Sometimes I wrote really large so there were fewer words on each page but I made sure to fill both pages with words."

Jeremy rolled his eyes. "Mom?"

"The chief is right. Write two whole pages of words."

"Fine. I'll copy it onto two new pages, in big print."

We watched Jeremy slink away before I turned to Sparky. "Thanks. It's good for Jeremy to hear rules from someone besides his mom and me."

Straightening himself, Sparky smiled. "I think that's why the guys elected me as the fire chief. I'm willing to speak up and enforce the rules. There are times when the guys would rather go home after a fire instead of hanging the hoses and cleaning the trucks. I keep after them to make sure everything is shipshape before we close the firehouse doors."

I stood and gathered the empty plates. "We're lucky to have you as the chief," I replied.

Standing uneasily at the end of the table, Sparky looked at Jenny. "Thanks for answering my questions about Wendy, Mrs. Rogers. I've been totally lost."

Jenny smiled as she stood. "You're a gentleman, Chief. Most guys would've forged ahead with their physical relationship. You're genuinely concerned about Wendy, being proper, and respecting boundaries. That's refreshing."

"Thanks again for supper. It's nice to have someone besides Mom to talk with. I can't really bring up my sex life over supper with her."

I carefully avoided offering to be Sparky's sounding board as I led him to the door. "I'm glad we could help you."

Stopping at the door, Sparky leaned close and whispered. "Chief Stone told me about the information you relayed about the bait shop fire having a different feel, probably because it was set by someone other than the arsonist from years ago."

"I imagine that old arsonist is dead."

"He was smart. I talked to the older firemen, who all said all those fires from years ago always looked accidental. There's no question the bait shop was torched by someone who dumped gas on the floor."

"Did the fire crew have any thoughts about who would do something like that?"

Sparky shook his head. "Not really. I mean, who knows an arsonist?"

"Yeah, that question comes up with every crime. I doubt Chief Stone ever interviews someone who tells him that their neighbor is a murderer or child molester. I'm sure they tell him their neighbor was quiet and kept to himself, but they never say, 'He's the killer. Arrest him!'"

"I wonder if there was someone the owner irritated. It's not like someone would torch the place because their minnows didn't catch fish."

Chapter 9

After hanging my jacket in my office and checking my email, I carried my coffee cup to the dining room to catch the end of the breakfast crowd. Half the residents had already eaten and moved on. Many who remained were socializing over coffee. Karla waved at me from halfway across the room as I drew a cup of coffee from the urn.

Nodding to people and patting shoulders, I walked to the table where Karla, Mary, and Kathy were seated. Their breakfast dishes had been cleared and they were drinking coffee. Kathy slid a chair back for me. "How was your frozen lasagna?"

Constantly amazed that something as trivial as what I'd prepared for supper had become common knowledge at the residence within twelve hours, I replied, "I prefer homemade, but the frozen dinners are quick and easier."

Mary smiled. "I'd go a step farther than that and say that take out was even simpler and doesn't heat up the kitchen."

Kathy waved off that comment. "Take out only works if you live close enough to town to drive to the restaurant. If you're farming, you prepare meals from scratch. It's cheaper and makes your family appreciate you."

Karla shook her head. "Not that I'm speaking from experience, but some families prefer a takeout or a frozen meal to our home cooking."

Kathy grinned at me. "Jenny says you're a pretty good cook, Peter. Now that she doesn't have to check the refrigerator to make sure the milk hasn't expired."

"My bachelor days are behind me. With two kids in the house, the milk is used up long before the expiration date arrives."

Kathy looked around to see if anyone was listening to us, then leaned close. "Did Sparky really stop over at your house for dating advice?"

"Where did you hear that rumor?" I asked.

The three women looked surprised at my question. "Jenny told us," Mary explained.

I shook my head. "We had a brief discussion with Sparky over supper."

Mary raised her eyebrows. "I heard that Sparky hasn't dated since high school. He's so caught up in being a fireman that he hasn't had time to date."

Kathy laughed. "It's more like he's spent so many nights drinking with the firemen that he hasn't had time to date."

Karla wasn't having any of those reasons. "I think it's got to be extremely difficult to cultivate a relationship when you're living with your mother. Where do you go for a romantic interlude?"

The three women looked at me as if I should have the answer. I shrugged and sipped my coffee. "That's a good question."

Hulda Packer entered the dining room and scanned the faces before seeing us. She banged her walker against chairs and ran over toes as she plowed a path toward our table. "Peter, you have to help Sparky," she announced.

"What does Sparky need help with?" I asked.

"He wants to make whoopee with Wendy, but he can't seem to make the arrangements. Don't you have a spare bedroom?"

"I'm not offering my spare bedroom for romantic interludes involving Sparky, Wendy, or anyone else."

Hulda gave me the stink eye. "You'd think you'd be trying hard to help out another veteran."

"Sparky was never in the service. He's not a veteran."

"He most certainly is a veteran. He still wears his uniform."

"Sparky wears a fireman's uniform. That doesn't make him a military veteran."

"Hmpf. Someone needs to give him a hand in the romance department. Wendy's patience is wearing thin. If she can't get him into the sack pretty soon, she's going to get prickly heat."

"Prickly heat?" I asked.

"You know, what women get when they start menopause."

Karla leaned forward. "I think you mean hot flashes. Wendy is probably a decade away from the onset of menopause and hot flashes."

Hulda pulled a tissue from her sleeve and dabbed at her nose. "I always called them prickly heat. It felt like my skin was on fire."

Trying to be rational with Hulda was an exercise in futility, but I tried anyway. "I treated a lot of Marines for heat rashes. We called that prickly heat when I was in Iraq."

Hulda's head jerked toward me. "You were in Iraq with a bunch of middle-aged women who had prickly heat?"

"No, I was in Iraq with a platoon of male Marines who got heat rashes."

"What's that got to do with prickly heat?" Hulda asked.

"Heat rashes are sometimes referred to as prickly heat."

"Bah!" Hulda said, swinging her walker around and banging it off my knees. "And I thought you were some kind of medical professional. I shouldn't have expected a musician to understand the problems of menopause."

We watched Hulda push past the nearby tables. Mary finally spoke. "It takes the patience of Job to deal with Hulda."

"No," Kathy said, "it takes good antidepressants."

Karla leaned close. "Did you discuss birth control with Sparky?"

I recoiled. "No, I *did not* discuss birth control with Sparky. I'm sure he understands the implications of intimacy."

Karla put her hand on my arm. "Think about that statement, Peter. We're talking about Sparky."

"Wendy is the more experienced partner in that relationship. I'm sure she can coach him through that as well as explain the intricacies of ladies' lingerie."

"What does he need to know about women's underwear?" Kathy asked.

I threw up my hands. "I don't know. He just asked if there have been any innovations or changes in women's undergarments in the past decade. I assured him that if Wendy wanted her undergarments removed that she'd either take care of it herself or coach him through it."

Kathy was laughing. "Sex was so much easier before the invention of Spanx and sports bras."

"I don't know," Karla said. "Girdles and corsets presented their own problems, in the day."

I stood. "It's been an interesting discussion, but I think it's time for me to leave."

Kathy put her hand on Karla's arm. "Pay up. I told you we could get Peter to blush."

Mary shook her head. "I didn't take the bet. I figured there was no way he'd get out of this conversation without being embarrassed."

I nearly ran over Wendy who was walking into the dining room with a crossword puzzle in one hand and a pencil in the other. "Peter, I need a three-letter word for an intimate relationship that starts with an S and ends in X."

"Not funny," I said as I stalked toward my office.

"What did you say to Sparky?" she asked as I walked away without replying.

* * *

I couldn't get Sparky and Wendy out of my mind as I considered Halloween entertainment. Senior citizen options were limited by not using sharp knives, mobility issues, my budget, and my current lack of inspiration. I typed in a search for senior citizen Halloween games. Bingo topped the list, followed by pumpkin bocce ball, and A-to-Z Halloween words.

Leaning back on my flimsy desk chair, I tried to list Halloween words that started with each letter of the alphabet and stalled after Halloween, pumpkin, and costume. I quickly made up a sheet with a column of letters, A-to-Z, with blank lines next to each letter.

Startled by the voice behind me, I turned as the printer created my sheet. Brian sat in my chair, peeking over my shoulder at the printer.

"I'm printing out a sheet for a Halloween word game."

"What kind of words are you looking for?" he asked.

"People will need to write in a Halloween word that starts with each letter of the alphabet." I handed the printout to him.

"Tuba," he said, handing the sheet back to me.

"How is tuba a Halloween-themed word?"

"I'll play the tuba during the Halloween concert."

"By that reasoning, all the band instruments could be listed."

"Yes."

"Yes, what?"

"All the band instruments are related to Halloween."

Deciding to change the conversation, I asked, "Don't you have a joke for me?"

A grin crept over Brian's face. "A ghoul showed up at the Halloween poker party. Pulling out a chair he said, 'I'm rigor mortis. May I set in?'"

I groaned out loud.

"I suppose that would be over your son's head."

"Rigor mortis hasn't come up during our dinner discussions."

Brian stood. "There you go. Something to talk about while you're eating pumpkin pie."

"That's it? You came here to see what I was doing and to tell a sick joke? Now you're going to leave?"

Snapping his finger and rolling his head like he'd forgotten something, Brian said,

"Meg needs your help tomorrow. The Lions Club needs help setting up for the pancake breakfast and she needs a judge for all the events."

"I am *not* the only chamber of commerce member who can do tasks."

"You're the only one who actually *does* stuff. All the rest show up at Judy's Café for the coffee and rolls. You actually participate after the plans are in place."

"I have a wife and kids."

Brian wiggled his eyebrows. "You're also gullible enough to answer the call to duty when Meg calls. The rest of us have blocked her phone number."

"That's not funny," I said to the empty door as Brian disappeared.

"What's not funny?" Jenny asked, showing up in the space Brian had occupied a moment before.

"Brian said the other chamber of commerce members have blocked Meg Cochran's phone number. That's why she keeps calling me to help."

"The alternate explanation would be that you're a civic-minded person who is polite, smart, and capable." Jenny paused. "Why don't you pick up a pizza on the way home. Cooking supper will be one less thing on your to do list."

Glancing at the clock, I recoiled. "It's quitting time already?"

"I'd like a veggie pizza. The kids like plain cheese pizza."

"I like the house special, with all the toppings."

Jenny cocked her head. "I don't think we need three pizzas, and it wouldn't kill you to eat a pizza that wasn't dripping grease."

"The flavor is in the grease," I protested.

"The flavor is in the sauce, sailor."

"I like leftover pizza."

Jenny grimaced. "All the grease congeals when it's cold."

"That's why God made microwave ovens."

"Do whatever you think is right," she said, turning to leave.

"I think that's unfair! I want to do what tastes good, not what's right."

Jenny's head reappeared in the door. "You abdicated that right when you said, 'I do.'"

"Giving up fun and not eating greasy foods were not in our wedding vows."

Jenny chuckled. "Other duties as assigned."

Chapter 10

Despite my best effort to eat breakfast quietly and sneak out of the house, the whole family came downstairs before I'd finished my toast and coffee. "Dad, can I come with you to the park?"

"I need to be there in a few minutes to set up tables for the Lions Club pancake breakfast and bingo."

"I'd rather have pancakes than cereal," Jeremy announced before racing upstairs to change out of his pajamas.

I gave Jenny a pleading look. "I need to work, not watch Jeremy."

"Go! I'll change Amy, then the three of us will drive over for pancakes and sausage."

I pecked Jenny on the cheek and rushed out of the door.

* * *

I parked at the Norwegian Lutheran Church and walked the two blocks to Owens Park where eight members of the Lions Club were erecting tents and setting up chairs. The aroma of cooking breakfast sausage filled the air. A second Lions Club crew had griddles heating. A few of the local people were already lined up for pancakes. Meg Cochran was talking with the Lions Club president as I approached.

"How can I help?" I asked as I approached Meg and Len Michaels.

Len pointed to the back of his minivan. "There are bottles of syrup and tubs of butter that need to be distributed to the tables."

Before I could take a step, Meg put her hand on my arm. "Thanks for pitching in. I know your family probably wants you to prepare for their Halloween activities."

"Jenny and the kids will be here to eat pancakes in a few minutes."

Meg nodded. "I understand if you need to be with them. On the other hand, I'm short workers and judges. I'll take whatever time you can offer."

"I think a lot of our family Halloween preparation involves Chief Stone's family. I will be free to do my civic duty."

Meg, who was usually highly professional, pulled me into an uncharacteristic hug. "I rarely tell you how much I appreciate you. Thanks."

After setting butter and syrup on all the tables, the pancake crew started serving the first people in line. Sherry Vogel nudged my shoulder. "Hi, Peter. Will you take one of these carafes and help me top off the coffee cups?"

Circling the tables, I poured coffee for people who gestured. Sherry worked toward me from the opposite side of the tables.

Meeting in the middle, we paused. "I'm not usually up this early," Sherry said, yawning.

"I'm surprised to see you."

"My mom flipped on my bedroom lights at 6:00 and told me to get my behind down here."

"I thought you lived in the UMD dorm."

Stifling another yawn, Sherry nodded. "I made the mistake of coming home to wash clothes last night. My mom is one of those early-to-bed, early to rise people. It kills her to let me sleep until 7:00."

"Ah, the price of doing laundry at home may exceed the monetary cost of the washers and dryers in the dorm."

Seeing someone gesturing for a coffee refill, Sherry nodded. "I ran out of quarters. And Mom washes for me if I'm busy." Then she dashed off to fill coffee cups.

I saw Jenny carrying Amy through the pancake serving line, so I set down my carafe to carry a plate for her. "Hi, sailor. Do you think you could assist a helpless girl carry her pancakes to a table?"

With his plate of pancakes and sausage, Jeremy looked up and shushed us. "Mom, you're embarrassing me." He rushed off to sit with some of his school friends, leaving me with Jenny and Amy.

I picked up two plates of pancakes and carried them to open seats near the end of a table. "Jeremy is reaching that irritating stage where he doesn't want to be seen with us," I said as we sat down.

Amy grabbed a sausage as Jenny sat down. "Wait, honey. I need to cut that up for you."

I quickly sliced some bite-sized pieces of pancake and poured syrup on them. "Try these, Amy."

"Peter, feed them to her. Don't let her eat them with her fingers!"

Amy was quicker than I was, and she snatched up a dripping piece of pancake and jammed it into her mouth. She looked smug as syrup ran down her hand and dripped onto Jenny's jeans.

"Oops," I said.

I got the look. "There are wet wipes in the bag."

"Do you want them now, or would you rather wait until the end of breakfast?"

"I'd like to wipe the syrup off my leg now. We'll need a bunch of them after Amy's through eating."

With Jenny's jeans wiped, I was about to eat a piece of pancake when Meg swept up to us with Sherry at her side. A master of managing people, Meg touched Jenny's shoulder. "I'm so sorry, but no one arranged for people to judge the pumpkin pie-tasting competition. Would it be terribly inconvenient if I stole Peter? I can team him up with Sherry and the police chief so we have three judges."

Knowing that she was being manipulated into agreeing, Jenny smiled at Meg. "Of course, you can take Peter. Amy and I will be fine."

Meg took my elbow and steered me toward the rear of the bandshell. "I can't believe that Linda Gustafson would find a dozen bakers to make pies, but not arrange for anyone to taste them."

"No problem," I replied, pulling the paper napkin from my lap and dropping it into a barrel as we raced past. "Are you up for this?" I asked Sherry.

"I didn't have time for breakfast, so I'm starving."

Kerry was waiting for us near a table where more than a dozen pumpkin pies were set out. A number was set next to each pie, and they'd been cut into slices. To the side, the entrants were grouped, looking proud.

Meg handed Kerry, Sherry, and me each a fork and a pen. "Put a slice of pie on a small paper plate, then taste a bite of it. There are clipboards with paper. Make notes by the numbers, but don't do any ranking. Once you've tasted all the pies, you should talk amongst yourselves and select the three or four best. Then, go back and resample the finalists before making your final vote on first, second, and third place."

Kerry leaned close to Meg's ear. "I don't like pumpkin pie."

Meg smiled and whispered, "Suck it up, Buttercup. You're a judge and you'll pick out the best."

"What if I don't like any of them?"

Meg closed her eyes, apparently counting to ten. "Then pretend they're all good and let the other judges choose the winner."

Nodding as if Meg had said something profound, Kerry leaned close. "Find another judge."

Sherry looked scared. I grinned, waiting to see how this battle of strong-willed people would play out. "Too late, chief. You're stuck."

Surprising all of us, Sherry called out. "Brian Johnson, come over here."

Meg glared at Sherry, then at Brian as he sauntered over. Undeterred, Sherry spoke loudly. "The chief has an emergency. Can you fill in as the third pie taster, Brian?"

Sensing that there was something amiss, Brian hesitated. "I suppose I can…"

Before Brian finished the sentence, Meg nudged Kerry away and pulled Brian close. "Do you like pumpkin pie?"

Thinking he was being asked a trick question, Brian glanced at Meg, Sherry, and the line of bakers. "It depends."

"Depends on what?" Meg whispered.

Brian nodded to the gathered bakers. "My wife submitted one of the pies. Can I recuse myself from voting on her pie?"

Meg nodded to Marybeth Johnson, Brian's wife.

"Can you identify her pie from the others?"

Brian surveyed the array of pies. "I'm not sure. I think Marybeth put her pie on a green plate."

"But you're not certain, are you," Meg coached.

Catching on, Brian smiled. "I'm not one hundred percent certain, but I have a strong suspicion that the middle pie on the green plate came from our house."

Meg hung her head. "At this point, I really don't care if you make yummy noises when you sample Marybeth's pie. Just be polite, smile as you sample each pie, and don't embarrass any of the bakers."

Brian smiled. "I can be the model of discretion." Smiling at his wife Brian whispered, "If Marybeth's pie doesn't win, do you have a spare bedroom, Peter?"

Sherry started coughing like she'd swallowed wrong. After a second, she took a deep breath and started laughing. "I've never heard a tuba player claim to be the model of discretion. You're usually telling the band off-color, tasteless jokes."

Still smiling at Marybeth, Brian added, "If I vote against my wife's pie, I may need to find a plumber who can remove a pie from my tuba."

Meg glared at us. "Can we get on with this?"

The trio of judges approached the table and sampled the first pie. Brian smiled and leaned close. "Are we supposed to make supportive comments now, like they do on that British baking show?"

Sherry smiled at the bakers. "I think we're supposed to act indifferent and talk seriously among ourselves."

Brian nodded. "Well, indifferently, I'd say the first pie is mediocre."

I bit my lip. "Write some noncommittal comments on your notepad. We're moving on."

The second pie was somewhat better. We didn't comment between ourselves, just making notes and moving on to the third pie. I took a bite and stopped after one chew. If I'd had a napkin, I would've spit it out.

Brian cocked his head. "What an unusual spice blend. Do I detect a bit of curry?"

Sherry's eyes started watering. "It's spicy. My whole mouth burns. I don't think I can swallow it."

Brian snorted. "You darned Swedes can't handle a bit of spice."

Swallowing, Sherry drew a breath. "My tastebuds are on fire. I don't know if I'll be able to taste anything the rest of the day."

I pointed to a pie that had been topped with whipped cream. "Let's jump ahead to number seven. The whipped cream will kill the burn."

Taking a big bite and holding the pie in her mouth, Sherry nodded and gave me a thumbs up. I leaned close to Brian and said, "We won't be including number three in our resampling."

Brian chuckled. "I think we should rule out any non-traditional recipes."

I pointed to the last pie. "Just so we don't give the impression of favoritism, I think we should sample the last pie, then jump around through the rest of the entries."

The sixth pie we tasted was the entry on the green plate. Brian made a point of not making eye contact with his wife as he ate his sample. "Is this Marybeth's recipe?" I asked.

"I think so. But I can't tell. I like it."

Sherry leaned close. "I still can't taste anything. Is this one good?"

Putting a hand to my forehead and not looking at the bakers I said, "Let's just move to number four, shall we."

After sampling the last pie, I gestured for Sherry and Brian to follow me to the end of the table farthest from the bakers. "Meg said we should go back and sample the three best. Look at your notes and tell me which three should be resampled."

Sherry studied her notes and whispered. "I couldn't taste any of the ones after the curry pie, so I'd have to say numbers one and two. Although, number seven was soothing, due to the whipped cream. Numbers two and eight were interesting because they had berries in them."

"Yes!" Brian exclaimed. "Marybeth puts lingonberries and cardamon in her pie. She calls her secret recipe a Swedish Thanksgiving pie."

Excusing herself from the other bakers, Brian's wife joined us. "Is Brian really one of the judges?"

"They dragged me in against my will," Brian protested.

Marybeth put out her hand to Sherry, then me. "I'm Brian's wife. To remove any perception of bias, I'm withdrawing my entry from the competition. I made number eight, on the green plate."

"I'm sure your pie is the winner," Brian said.

"You're off the hook, dear," Marybeth replied. Then she walked to the table and removed her entry from the group.

"Who does that leave as the finalists?" I asked.

Brian looked at his notes. "I liked two, five, and eleven."

Checking my notes I said, "Two, five, and nine were my choices."

Sherry shrugged. "I guess two is the best of the ones I could taste. I kind of liked seven because it was covered with whipping cream that stopped the burning."

Walking to the table of pies I looked at my notes. "The finalists are pies number two, five, seven, and eleven. We're going to resample those four, and announce the first, second, and third place pies."

After resampling, I consulted Brian and Sherry. "Well?"

"I like the one with the berries," Sherry said. "My vote is for number two."

Brian nodded. "I think number two is best. Five is my choice for second place. Third place is a toss-up."

I returned to the pie table. "First place is number two. Second place is number five. Third place is number nine."

The numbered paper slips were flipped over, revealing the names of the winners. Most of the entrants congratulated Ardys Christenson, the winner. A couple of the women hung back and were less pleased with the result.

A woman approached me and took me aside. "I was hopeful that my Indian-inspired recipe might excite the judges."

"I'm afraid the judges preferred the traditional recipes," I replied.

The woman sighed. "Maybe I'll try for Polynesian next year. You might really like pineapple and coconut pumpkin pie."

I watched the woman pick up pie number three and leave as Kerry nudged me away from the crowd. "I spoke with Bud Oldham, the bait shop owner. He has a rock-solid alibi for the fire. I pointed out that it might be so solid that it was suspicious."

"I take it that most people don't know what they were doing at a specific time."

Kerry nodded. "It's very convenient that he'd been bowling, with about fifty witnesses, when the fire broke out. He felt badly about Speedy Antonich dying in the fire. The bait shop was one of Speedy's hangouts. There were several old-timers who hung out there drinking coffee and lying about past fishing and hunting adventures. Speedy had been there until Bud locked up the afternoon of the fire. Speedy purchased a box of 16-gauge shotgun shells but forgot to take them when he left. Bud left them sitting on the counter when he closed up. He speculated that Speedy went back to pick them up, found the door unlocked, and walked in on the arsonist."

"Do you think that's a likely scenario?"

Kerry shrugged. "It's as likely as any other I can dream up. Bud was really broken up over Speedy's death. If Bud was responsible for the fire, Speedy's death was not part of the plan."

"Now what?" I asked.

"We keep digging," Kerry replied before walking away.

Meg was engaged in a heated discussion with one of the Lions Club men with her back to us. I caught snippets of their conversation about the pancake batter running out while there were still people lined up for breakfast. I tried to interrupt, hoping to announce the end of the pie tasting, when I was distracted by the bakers. Most were chatting among themselves. The person who'd prepared the pie with whipped cream, looked unhappy as she lifted her pie from the table. The target of her displeasure appeared to be Brian, who was telling his Halloween jokes to a man I recognized as a trombone player from the band.

To my horror, the woman marched toward Brian with the pie balanced in one hand. Pie fight scenes from "The Three Stooges" movies flashed through my mind as I moved to intercept the woman before Brian got a pie in the face. Unable to wade through the crowd, I yelled a warning. "Look out!"

Brian heard the warning and stepped aside as the woman cocked her arm and launched the pie. My warning shout alerted a number of people. Rather than ducking, they all turned toward me to see why I'd shouted. Meg, who had been standing with her back to Brian, turned toward me just in time for the pie to glance off her shoulder and splatter her face with pumpkin filling and whipped cream.

Sensing the magnitude of her errant plan to hit Brian with the pie, the baker turned and fled while everyone else looked on in horror. Sherry Vogel, who'd been watching from the side, snatched a dish towel from the pie display table and stepped forward to wipe pie remnants from Meg's face.

With her bare hand, Meg wiped a glob of pie from her cheek and flung it to the ground. Accepting the towel, Meg wiped her face and did something unexpected. She started laughing.

"Thanks for the warning, Peter," she said as she wiped the pumpkin and whipped cream from her ear. "Next time, try yelling 'duck' instead of 'look out.'"

"I didn't have any time to choose my warning."

"Was I the intended target?" Meg asked.

Sherry shook her head. "I think one of the contestants was irritated with Brian and his wife over the selection of the winners."

Brian picked pie crust from Meg's shoulder. "I'm sorry, Meg. I would've happily taken a pie to my face to save you."

Chuckling, Meg shook her head. "Sure, you would have, Brian. Just like my personal protection squad, you would've taken a bullet to protect me."

"Not a bullet, but I would've stepped in front of you to block a pie or cake. Actually, I'd block any pastry thrown at you."

A cheer went up at the north end of the park, and someone lifted an intricately carved pumpkin over her head. Sherry stepped next to me. "I want to judge pumpkin carving and not the pies next year."

Chapter 11

The crowd watching the pumpkin carving started to move away. Art Christenson, the Chamber of Commerce secretary, rushed over to Meg and whispered in her ear. She turned, scanned the crowd, then grabbed my elbow. "I need a judge at the football field for the pumpkin cannon contest, right now!"

My first thought was, *Isn't there anyone else?* Then I realized that being in the front line of the first-ever pumpkin shooting contest might be interesting. "Am I going to be the only judge?" I asked, hoping that having a second judge might provide deniability if there was a disputed measurement.

Meg glanced around the crowd of people. "Sherry, you volunteered to help with whatever I needed. Go with Peter."

I chuckled and glanced at Sherry, who was smiling. "Is this the public service part of Sherry's penance?"

Waving off my question, Meg shook her head. "Sherry is a willing helper and people like her are few and far between."

Art handed me small red flags glued to wooden dowels from a shopping bag. "Use these to mark the pumpkin landings."

Reluctantly, I accepted the flags. "I think the pumpkins themselves will be evidence of where they land."

"Humor me, Peter," Art replied. "Personally, I think the whole cannon event is going to be a bust. Maybe the flags will add drama to the event if a pumpkin ever makes it out of one of the cannon barrels."

Several school buses were lined up to shuttle people from downtown to the high school, where the cannons were being set up. A friendly family let Sherry and me cut in line ahead of them when we said we were the event judges.

"What are we going to judge?" Sherry asked as we shuffled toward the bus. "The pumpkin that flies the farthest, wins."

"Do we mark where the pumpkin hits, or where it stops rolling?"

Sherry cocked her head. "You don't expect the pumpkins to roll, do you? I think they'll break open when they hit the ground."

"Okay, do we measure where they impact, or the end of the splatter?"

Sherry giggled. "You're so funny, Peter. I don't think there will be any controversy."

I raised an eyebrow. "Do you remember the lutefisk toss at the Tall Ships Festival? There were rolling lutefisk lumps."

Sherry giggled, "The whole downtown reeked of lutefisk until a thunderstorm washed the lutefisk slime into the lake."

"I'm afraid we'll have a situation where the results are ambiguous."

We shuffled onto the bus, then found a seat about halfway back. Sherry settled in next to me and smiled. "You're a nut. I'm glad Meg teamed us up."

"Thanks for being a good sport. I'm surprised that the Svenska Gotters aren't protesting the Halloween festivities. Their beliefs run contrary to the Halloween witches, ghosts, and goblins."

"Shh," Sherry hissed, looking around to see if anyone had overheard me. She leaned close. "Meg was very cagey. She asked my mom if I could help with the harvest festival."

"Really? You don't think that they have connected the October 31 festival with Halloween?"

"There's something about Meg's approach to things that disarms people. She's been very good to me. We've spoken at length about my modeling and how college has allowed me to blossom from under the shadow of Dad's congregation. Meg's a very special person."

"She is. Somehow, she gets me to volunteer for all kinds of community events while making it seem like it was my idea."

Sherry slid closer to me and whispered, "Today has been the most pleasant part of my penance. It beats the heck out of picking litter off Highway 61 from here to Duluth. Thank you."

"You're great company, Sherry. I'd be happy to have you as my partner any time."

"I would like some clarinet lessons before next year's band season."

"Let me know when you're off school over Christmas break. I'll make some time for you."

"Won't your wife be unhappy about you giving private lessons to a college girl?"

"Jenny knows that when I said, 'I do,' it meant forever. She has nothing to be jealous about."

"Peter Rogers, you are the strangest, and nicest man I know."

"Thanks, that means a lot to me."

"Is it true that you're helping Chief Stone investigate the bait shop fire?"

I sighed. "I'm more of a consultant. I talk with the people at Whistling Pines to get a historical background."

"My mom says that a business burns down every ten years under suspicious circumstances. She thinks people are burning their stores down so they can collect the insurance money, then retire."

"Do you believe that?"

Sherry's brow wrinkled as she thought. "I don't think so. Mr. Antonich died in the bait shop, and he had nothing to do with that business. He was just a nice old guy. Did you know that he used to bring his skates to the ice rink every afternoon? He played hockey with anyone who was there."

"Really? A guy who'd won several professional hockey championships would play with the kids at the ice rink?"

"He always played for the girl's team because he felt we needed extra help."

"Did he score a lot of goals for you?"

"He never scored a single goal. He always passed the puck to one of us, so we got the shot. He made us all better. I'm really sad that he's gone."

"Is there anyone in town who didn't like him?"

Sherry chuckled. "All the boys were irritated with him because he helped the girls. But it's not like anyone would kill him over pick-up hockey games."

"What else was Mr. Antonich into besides hockey?"

"It's not like any of us really knew him. He'd show up at games and tell us stories about playing in the NHL. I don't even know if he was married or had kids."

The bus stopped at the old football field, near Skunk Creek and the campground. Ahead of us the aroma of food filled the air where a row of vendors sold everything from bratwurst to tiny doughnuts. Beyond the campground, which was filled with camper trailers and tents, was Lake Superior.

We got off the bus and Sherry inhaled deeply. "The doughnut aroma is making my mouth water."

I looked at the dozen people in line at the doughnut vendor and shook my head. "I think we've got to check out the cannon and pumpkin situation."

Mounted on a hay wagon, Cliff Berggren's cannon was constructed from PVC pipe. An air compressor hummed nearby, ready to provide propulsion for the cannon. Cliff, wearing bib overalls over a plaid shirt, looked the part of a farmer, right down to his green cap advertising John Deere tractors.

Burt Halstrom's cannon, constructed from pieces of metal pipe he'd welded together, was mounted on a trailer large enough to transport a car. Two propane cylinders were mounted on the front of the trailer, ready to provide propellant to the cannon. From his greasy jeans to the short-brimmed cap often worn by pipefitters and steam engineers, Burt's outfit fit his occupation as machine shop owner,

I led Sherry to the trailers where the competitors were sorting through a pile of pumpkins, trying to find those that would fit into their cannon muzzles. "Are you guys almost ready?" I asked.

Burt nodded, then smiled at Cliff. "He hasn't got a chance with that toy cannon."

Hefting a pumpkin about six inches in diameter, Cliff scoffed. "It's all about physics, Burt. Oh, that's right. You flunked physics class."

Burt's cannon was smaller in diameter, but he held up a pumpkin that appeared to match the diameter of the cannon's bore. "There's no theoretical physics involved in this, Cliff. It's all about the beefier construction of my cannon. It looks like your peashooter will self-destruct the first time you fire it."

Casey Johnson, the high school media arts teacher, climbed onto Burt's trailer with a microphone. The amps shrieked with feedback, then settled down when Casey adjusted the volume. "Burt, tell us about your cannon."

"It's pretty simple. I've got a ten-inch diameter ignition chamber that gets filled with propane. It's got a spark plug igniter, and it'll launch a pumpkin like you've never seen before."

Casey stepped up onto the hay wagon and introduced Cliff. "How does your cannon work, Cliff?"

"I'm using an air compressor with a five-gallon pressure tank." He feigned scorn by glancing at Burt's propane cannon. "I think my cannon will fire the pumpkin out of the muzzle while barely using a fraction of the compressor's 150 psi capability."

I motioned Burt over. "We're supposed to judge the competition. How far is your cannon going to shoot the pumpkin?"

Burt laughed. "I have no idea. We fired it against the cement block wall of the building a couple of times and it splattered the pumpkins impressively. But I have no idea what that means in terms of distance."

I looked down the football field, then at the campground beyond. Past the campground was a couple hundred miles of Lake Superior. "Are we talking about part of the football field distance, or are you going to lob a pumpkin into the lake?"

Burt looked down the field. "I'll just give it a little shot of propane. The pumpkin won't make it past the far goalpost."

"Have you talked to Cliff about distance?" I asked.

"Yeah. He's only going to give it 10-15 psi. I told him that might not be enough to push the pumpkin out of the barrel. He assured me that he's done the math."

I hopped down, where Sherry looked at me expectantly. "Well?"

"Let's go down to the fifty-yard line. I don't think they'll go farther than that."

Casey flapped his arms, trying to rev up the crowd as Cliff ran up the air pressure in his tank. "Here we go! Fifteen pounds!"

He threw open a valve and the cannon shuddered before the pumpkin emerged followed by a "pop." The pumpkin traveled past the end of the hay wagon but didn't even roll to the nearest goal line.

The crowd roared, and Cliff tore off his hat and beat it against his leg, putting on a great show of disgust and disappointment. Sherry put out her hand for a flag. "Aren't we going to mark where the pumpkin hit?"

"If that's the longest shot, this whole event will be a bust."

The crowd ate up Cliff's overly dramatic antics as Casey carried the mic to Burt. "Can you beat that, Burt?"

Burt snorted then flipped a valve that let some propane into the ignition chamber. He leaned close to the microphone. "If this doesn't fly fifty yards; I'll eat my hat." Pressing an ignition switch caused the pumpkin to fly out of the cannon at a high trajectory. The cannon made a boom that reminded me of a firework going off. The pumpkin flew, landing about seventy yards down the field, where it broke into pieces.

The crowd roared as Sherry raced down the field with a flag to mark the pumpkin impact point. It was unnecessary because the pumpkin had broken into large chunks upon landing.

Cliff waved his hat to get Casey's attention. "I think we should go for the best two out of three shots."

Casey turned to the crowd. "What do you think, folks? Should we go for the best of three attempts?" The crowd whooped and whistled their agreement.

Cliff walked into the assortment of remaining pumpkins, making a big show out of examining the size of the pumpkins and hefting them to compare their weight. After a few moments, he climbed onto the hay wagon and used a mop to shove the pumpkin down his cannon's barrel. He made a show of putting on a pair of safety goggles and a helmet before opening the valve to the pressure tank and acting like it was about to explode. It only took a few seconds to fill the tank to whatever pressure he'd chosen. He stepped back, flipped the valve and the pumpkin flew out of the barrel with a pop. It arced through the air and landed near the closest forty-yard line.

Sherry raced out with her flag as Berggren put on a great show of stomping around and shaking his fist at the cannon.

Burt Halstrom got into the showmanship, spending at least four or five minutes examining and lifting pumpkins until he acted surprised to find the perfect pumpkin. He climbed onto the trailer, lowered the cannon's barrel, and shoved the pumpkin into the barrel using a hydraulic ram that looked like it had once been a log splitter. Raising the barrel, he made a show of releasing propane into the ignition chamber. Apparently unhappy with the first release, he reopened the valve and added a bit more. Waving his arms to whip up the crowd, he waited until everyone was cheering, then pushed the ignition switch which launched the pumpkin even higher and farther than his first attempt.

Sherry took another flag and sprinted to the far ten-yard line, marking the ninety-yard shot.

Shaking his head, Cliff Berggren hopped down from the hay wagon and chose another pumpkin, repeating the loading process, and apparently filling his pressure chamber to a higher pressure. He waved his arms, whipping up his supporters. With the crowd cheering, he flipped the valve...and nothing happened. He quickly checked the pressure indicators and blew more compressed air into the cannon. The crowd waited, then the cannon emitted a mechanical groan.

Sherry tugged on my arm. "I don't like the sound of that. Shouldn't we run...or something?"

I was thinking the same thing and was ready to bolt when the air cannon emitted a loud popping sound. A pumpkin emerged from the barrel amid a puff of steam. The crowd cheered as the pumpkin arched into the sky. High over our heads the pumpkin reached the zenith of its arc as it continued flying toward the school. Past the football field, the trajectory changed. Then, barely over the nearest edge of the campground, the pumpkin arced down. I grabbed Sherry's arm and pulled her to the hay wagon where we had a better view of the upcoming impact.

Anticipating the disaster, Casey yelled into the microphone, warning campers that the pumpkin was about to fall into the campground. Campers ran. People screamed. The crowd around the cannons cheered, not fully cognizant of the impending danger posed by a twenty-pound pumpkin traveling at one hundred miles an hour.

Then, the pumpkin arced into a group of tents. A second later, a green tent billowed, followed by the sound of ripping fabric.

From my perch on the hay wagon, I saw over the crowd and watched the pumpkin strike the tent, rather high on the side facing the cannon. The tent was jerked, its anchoring stakes flying into the air, spewing dirt as they were ripped from the ground. A woman screamed, and a moment later I saw her naked butt racing away as she pulled a purple Minnesota Vikings sweatshirt over her head.

A moment later, a bearded naked man stood up in the hole that had been ripped in the tent wall. He stared at the crowd apparently dumbfounded, as the now semi-naked woman dashed away from the tent. A voice near me yelled, "That's Ralph McClaren!"

Someone else added, "I think the woman who's running away is his neighbor, Chloe Mikrot!"

With his shock fading, McLaren must've felt a breeze on his bare skin which made him look down. Realizing that he was naked, and still partially excited, he reached for the torn edge of the tent and pulled it up to his waist. Someone in the crowd yelled, "Hey Ralph, looks like your affair with Chloe is no longer a poorly kept secret!"

I couldn't think of a thing to do that would rectify the situation, so I decided to ignore the naked couple. I turned to jump down from the hay wagon when I bumped into Sherry, who was staring at the campground. "Is that what happened when you walked into the art class by accident?" she asked me.

"What do you mean?"

"It's kind of hard to look away when you're suddenly confronted by the sight of a naked person. I mean, the pumpkin kind of caused...coitus interruptus."

"I didn't notice."

Sherry cocked her head. "You didn't know I was posing for the art class. You walked in expecting the students to be painting fruit or something, and there I sat, naked.”

“I maintained eye contact with you the entire time.”

Sherry frowned. “You did. That was really professional. When I unexpectedly saw that naked guy, my eyes were immediately drawn to...”

“This is a totally different situation. Ralph is half a football field away, and gazing in that direction, you immediately took in his entirety.”

“Yeah, his entirety was sticking straight out.”

Thankfully, my discussion with Sherry was interrupted when Burt took the microphone from Casey and climbed atop the hay wagon. “Okay folks, we’ve proved that propane is a better pumpkin propellant. BUT, we haven’t seen just how far it can shoot a pumpkin! Would anyone like to see how far we can shoot a pumpkin into Lake Superior?”

The crowd roared and Burt jumped down to select another pumpkin from the pile. Sherry looked at me, then at the football field, the campground beyond the endzone, then the lake beyond that. She leaned close. “Peter, I don’t think this is a good idea.”

Lacking any engineering background, I shrugged. “Burt seems confident that he can launch a pumpkin all the way to the lake.”

Sherry watched Burt set the pumpkin on the hay wagon. Using a tire as a step, he hopped onto the wagon's bed. "Mr. Berggren thought he knew what was going to happen."

Considering Sherry's concern, the path of the pumpkin, the distance it needed to travel to go past the football field and the campground, made me anxious. I tried to push my way through the crowd to reach Burt. I thought he might listen to reason and stop the attempt.

With people all around me, I caught glimpses of the pumpkin preparation. I was intrigued as Casey wrapped the pumpkin in cheesecloth, then painted it with a white material from a bucket. As I pushed closer, Burt and Casey struggled to lift the white coated pumpkin to the cannon's muzzle. At one point, it slipped from their hands and nearly fell to the wagon bed. Judging by the laughter of the crowd and cannon loaders, I sensed something more at play than a simple pumpkin launch. The closer I got to the cannon, the rowdier and more densely packed the crowd became. By the time I reached the wagon, Burt was raising the muzzle skyward.

Pulling myself onto the wagon, my hand hit the bucket. I stared in horror at a bucket of lard with a paintbrush sticking out of the open top. I yelled for Burt to wait, but there was no way I could be heard over the increasingly excited crowd. To my horror, Burt opened a valve, feeding propane into the ignition chamber. I was scrambling across the hay wagon, hoping to stop him before he launched the lard-covered pumpkin. I was a step too late. He pressed the ignitor as I reached out to stop him. The cannon roared, and I was knocked to the wagon bed as the flaming pumpkin, trailing a tail of burning lard, arced over the football field toward the lake.

I looked at Burt, who seemed as surprised as I was. "Geez, who'd have thought the lard would ignite!"

The crowd went crazy, cheering and hooting as the fireball flew toward Lake Superior like a meteor. At some point, the public address man realized that there were small boats not far offshore that might be in danger. Shouting a warning, the announcer tried to get the attention of the boaters. The trajectory of the fireball was clear once it passed the shoreline. One fishing boat in particular was in jeopardy. Focused on his fishing rods, the boat's owner wasn't responding to the crowd or the public address. Apparently focused on his fishing gear, he slowly trolled across the unusually calm lake surface. We watched in horror as the fireball arced toward his boat. The crowd went silent in the seconds before the impending impact. We all held our breath as the fireball fell toward the boat and the clueless fisherman.

It appeared that the pumpkin had hit the boat until the geyser of water arose just past the boat's stern. The fisherman apparently noticed the fireball a second before it hit the water. First, he shielded his head with his forearm, then he was transfixed on the impact spot a few feet from the boat where the fireball caused a geyser of water.

"Sweet baby Jesus," a male voice said behind me. "I'll bet Ole quits drinking for good after that."

Someone else chuckled. "The pink elephants didn't do it. I'm sure he'll be telling everyone he was nearly hit by a meteor."

I stepped next to Burt, who was wiping his hands on a rag to remove the lard. "You're done, right?"

Sighing, Burt nodded. "I think we've adequately proven the power of propane versus an air compressor."

"I was thinking more about the liability," I replied. "Sinking a boat would have been bad."

"Yeah, even interrupting a campground romantic interlude was...risky."

Sensing Sherry beside me, I gestured for her to jump down from the hay wagon. "We should get back to town."

As we walked toward the shuttle buses, Sherry couldn't let go of the topic of the camper exposed by the pumpkin demolishing his tent. "It's not like I've seen many naked men, but that was educational."

"Yeah, I suppose ministers' daughters aren't exposed to that sort of thing."

Sherry giggled. "We're supposed to be surprised on our wedding night."

"Well, that's the approach your church prefers."

"Were you surprised on your wedding night?"

I stopped and pulled Sherry aside. "You should be having this discussion with your mother, not me."

"Are you kidding? My mother would drop over dead if she thought I'd seen a naked man. No, she'd kill me, then herself."

"You said that Meg has been like a mother to you. Talk to Meg."

"But I like talking to you, Peter. You're rational and I know what I say isn't going to be repeated."

Seeing the buses, I gestured for Sherry to follow me. "You and I shouldn't be having this conversation. It's not appropriate."

"What? It's not like we are naked, Peter. We're fully dressed, in a crowd of people, and having a conversation like mature adults."

"I've got news for you, Sherry. Mature adults don't have discussions about staring at naked body parts with members of the opposite sex old enough to be their parents. It's not appropriate."

"Peter, you're not old enough to be my father. Wait, you're blushing."

"Let's get on the bus and start a new conversation."

Sherry sat next to me and stared. I glanced at her grin and looked away. "What?"

"You're really embarrassed."

"Shh. If you have to talk to someone about this, talk to my wife. Jenny's a nurse. She's a more appropriate resource."

"Peter, it's not like we're planning a whatever."

"Shh. Talk about something else. How about those Vikings? What do you think of their chances of making it to the Superbowl this year?"

Sherry thought for a few moments. "I remember when you and Wendy were singing in the park, and you brought Jenny onstage. Tell me what it felt like to sing the duet with your wife in the bandshell."

"It was spontaneous. We just sang."

"You did NOT just sing. You were outside your body. Your eyes were closed and the whole crowd felt it. I've never had a surreal experience like that. What's it like?"

"I don't know how to describe it. I'm not playing the guitar, it's part of me. And the song just flows. I'm not remembering words, it's like they're being channeled to me. And when it's over, I'm exhausted. I've given everything to the crowd and my partner."

"I want to feel that sometime."

"It's not something you can plan on. It just happens. Part of being a musician is mastering your instrument, so you don't have to read the music. When you reach a certain point, the music just flows from your fingers."

"Wow."

"Janis Joplin said she made love to 10,000 people a night. She gave them every ounce of energy and herself."

Sherry's smile disappeared. "I remember that quote. 'I make love to 10,000 people a night, then go to bed alone.'"

"That's the nature of baring your soul to the crowd. You're touching each of them, giving yourself to them, then walking away feeling hollow and spent."

"That's why rock musicians get into drugs, isn't it?"

"It's hard to play the last song of the last set, then walk away. Your adrenaline has been pumping for an hour or two, and then you realize that you have to get up in the morning and go to a job. I think it's really easy to fall prey to uppers and downers so they can get ready for a concert every evening, then need something to sleep afterwards. I think that's why a lot of rock legends died of drug overdoses."

"How do you deal with that, Peter?"

"It's a make-believe world. The more you stay anchored in the real world, the less likely it is that you'll get sucked into the make-believe musical world. I have a family and a job that anchors me. Music is a hobby, not my life. I love playing, but afterwards I walk off the stage into my wife's arms and I tuck my children into bed."

"It seems so glamorous."

"Trust me, it's not. Travelling around in a tour bus, sleeping on the bus or in hotel rooms 200 nights a year, performing for cheering fans who only love you as long as you have a song in the top ten, people who want to exploit your talent, fame, and money, it's all a big bubble that's ready to pop."

"That's sad."

"Fall in love with a nice guy. Raise a family and go to PTA meetings. That's what real life is about. That's where I've found solid ground and happiness."

The bus stopped near the park and the doors opened. Sherry surprised me by leaning forward and kissing my cheek. "You're incredible, Peter. Your wife is so lucky."

I patted Sherry's shoulder. "No, I'm the lucky one."

Chapter 12

With the pumpkin cannon fiasco over, I was ready to meet my family back by the pie eating contest, then call it a day. Sherry Vogel followed me around like a lost puppy, bumping into me each time I stopped to look for Jenny and the kids.

"Sheesh, Sherry. Don't you need to be somewhere?"

"Actually, I'm trying to avoid the Svenka Gotters."

"Why?"

"They're kind of anti-Halloween and I'm trying to avoid a confrontation."

A gravelly male voice distracted me. "Have you found that arsonist yet?"

Darrell Sanders, a gruff Whistling Pines resident, stared at me through thick glasses. "The police chief is handling the investigation," I replied.

"That's not the story I heard."

"Chief Stone has it under control." I looked around. "Right now, I'm trying to find Jenny and my kids."

"I heard that my kid's place was going to be torched next."

I turned toward Darrell and frowned. "You should tell Chief Stone."

"I'm not supposed to know. That's why I'm telling you."

I noticed Sherry staring, waiting to hear my response. Feeling like I should act like a responsible adult in front of Sherry, I put aside my reluctance to become further involved in the arson investigation. "Who is your son? What business does he own?"

"You've never heard of Bruce's Body Shop?" Darrell asked.

Searching my memory for the location of a car body repair shop, I drew a blank. "Sorry. Is it located in Two Harbors?"

Sherry leaned against my shoulder and whispered, "It's the downtown exercise place."

"I told my idiot son to get out of the exercise business and open something like a bar that attracts customers," Darrell said, shaking his head. "But no, he says he can't keep up with the mortgage by catering to those bar patrons. As long as those damn exercise idiots want to run on treadmills instead of actually working for a living, his profits keep skyrocketing. You'd think that people would figure out that walking on the sidewalk is free."

Seeing the conversation straying far from the arson discussion, I tried to pull it back. "What makes you think someone is targeting your son's business?"

"Isn't it obvious?" Darrell asked. "It's one of the anti-gun wackos who burned down the bait shop. Next, it will be some couch potato who is anti-exercise and fed up watching the people running on treadmills in front of the windows overlooking the sidewalk. Have you ever noticed that none of the people in the front row are over thirty? All of them are good looking and none of them have an ounce of body fat. It's like they hide the flabby old folks out of sight in the back."

"Do you have evidence that any of the anti-gun people were involved in the bait shop fire?" I asked, hoping to return the conversation to arson.

Darrell huffed. "It doesn't take a rocket scientist to connect the dots. The bait shop sold guns and it was burned down. The Body Shop is next."

Feeling the sanity slipping away from the conversation, I looked around for someone who could throw water on the whole anti-exercise conspiracy theory. I looked at Sherry, who shrugged. "I'd join The Body Shop if I had a sedentary job."

Darrell nodded. "You'd be right up front. You're cute and in shape."

Seeing Sparky, I waved him over. "Darrell thinks the bait shop was burned down because of their gun sales. Can you set him straight?"

I knew I was in trouble before I'd completed the sentence. Sparky's eyes lit up and he started bobbing his head. "I hadn't considered that anti-minnow motive. I wonder how the Svenska Gotters feel about minnows and worms? Is there a chance they'd picket a bait shop?"

Seeing humor in Sparky's misdirection, Sherry giggled, "I think a lot of my dad's congregation are fishermen. I doubt they'd picket a bait shop."

Her comment drew Sparky's attention to her, and recognition swept over him. "Aren't you the nude model who's Pastor Vogel's daughter?"

Blushing, Sherry nodded, but didn't speak.

Sparky puffed up and spoke too loudly for the crowded conditions in the park. "I've got to hand it to you, Sherry. You've got a character. Standing up to the Svenska Gotters like you did over your nude modeling, that took some brass balls."

Half a dozen people turned to look at us after Sparky's exclamation. Sherry shrunk behind me as her face turned a deep crimson.

"Don't hide behind Peter Sparky said. "Hell, you should run for mayor or the county board. This town needs some people like you who are willing to stand up for what they believe in, even if that means sitting naked in front of an audience."

"Um, Sparky," I said, trying to get him to tone down his rhetoric. "You're embarrassing Sherry."

"With a cute body like hers, she's got nothing to be embarrassed about!"

"You've never seen her naked," I said.

"I saw the paintings!"

Darrell shook his head. "If you saw Hulda's painting, you'd have a hard time telling if the subject was fruit, a landscape, or a person."

"Well," Sparky said, "people sure thought a lot of Kathy Christensen's paintings. I think the nude painting of Sherry won first prize at the county fair!"

Sherry's eyes got large, and she looked at me. "A painting of me was displayed at the county fair?"

Not sensing Sherry's horror, Sparky smiled. "Oh, yah, there were a lot of folks who admired that painting."

Sherry grabbed my arm and asked, "Could they tell it was me?"

Trying to be reassuring, I said, "Kathy painted a rather generic woman's face on the nude body. As I recall, the model wasn't recognizable as anyone in particular."

Still clueless, Sparky added, "I don't think anyone was focused on the model's face."

A crowd was starting to gather, and Sherry slid behind me. It was time to change the topic. "Sparky, do you think there's any risk of someone burning down The Body Shop?"

Not the sharpest knife in the drawer, Sparky was quickly diverted to the new topic. "Risk? Of course, there's risk! Hell, there are all kinds of chubby people who hate that place and the hard-bodied folks who exercise in their front window. There's a lot of anti-fitness sentiment in this town. If you mention the exercise place in any of the local bars, you'll get an earful."

Tipping my head back, I closed my eyes and hoped for a lightning strike to hit us so the inane conversations could end. Sherry had buried her face between my shoulder blades. I couldn't think of a safe topic to divert Sparky.

The VFW manager came to my rescue. Vern tapped Sparky's shoulder and gestured at the growing crowd. "I think the crowd has exceeded the posted capacity of the park. I think you need to disperse them so there won't be a dangerous stampede if a fire breaks out in the bandshell."

Looking around, Sparky nodded. "Uff da. We could kill some people if there was a stampede." Sparky raised his hands over his head and gestured for people to move away.

Afraid that Sparky would overreact, I whispered, "Just make a path through the crowd so I can escort Sherry out of the park."

Gesturing emphatically, Sparky parted the crowd. "Everyone please back up. Please make a path for the nude model. Let her through."

"What nude model?" A voice called from the back of the crowd.

Ignoring the pressing crowd, I pulled Vern close. "Sherry is behind me. I'll walk toward the Lutheran Church. Stay behind Sherry and make sure we don't get separated."

"Go," he replied.

It took several minutes for us to get clear of the crowd and into the church parking lot. Sherry was shaking as Vern and I led her to the front steps. "What was Sparky thinking?" Vern asked.

"I don't think Sparky does a lot of thinking." Realizing that Sherry was close to tears, I took her hands and squeezed them. "You're safe."

"I'm not safe!" Sherry looked back at the park. "All those people think I'm a loose woman because I modeled for the art class."

Vern stepped in front of Sherry and looked at her earnestly. "They're a bunch of small-minded people who live in a small town. You're bigger than this."

Sherry pointed past Vern at the crowd around Sparky. "I have to live here with those people!"

"Don't you live in a Duluth dormitory?" Vern asked.

"Yes."

"Peter and I will walk you to your car. Drive back to Duluth and enjoy an evening with your friends. Don't give today another thought. Okay?"

Sherry nodded. Vern and I provided an escort to her car, parked a few blocks away. As she drove away Vern said, "That poor kid is a mess. She's walking a fine line between being a conservative minister's daughter and living a life as an open-minded artist."

"Families are tough," I replied.

Vern broke out laughing. "Do you mean like your mother, the left-wing wacko?"

"She's certainly one example."

"Has she ever forgiven you for joining the Navy?"

"I think everything was forgiven when I adopted Jeremy and her granddaughter was born."

Chapter 13

I'd barely hung up my jacket behind my office door when Sherry appeared. Unprepared for her sudden arrival, I must've frowned.

"I'm sorry if I'm interrupting," she said. "Do you want me to leave?"

Gesturing to my guest chair, I shook my head. "Your arrival surprised me. You drove all the way from Duluth this morning to see me?"

"I spent the night at my parents' house." She eased into the chair, looking deflated.

"Are you okay?"

She sighed. "I'm not entirely sure. I'm going to graduate at the end of this semester, and I have no idea what I'm going to do. Who hires art majors with a B.A. degree?"

"You need to talk to a counselor at school. I'm sure they can direct you to a career or additional training that will qualify you for a position."

"I thought I'd graduate, then move home and paint."

"Where did you plan to sell your paintings?"

Sherry shrugged. "I suppose at the Two Harbors art studio. I really hadn't thought that through entirely."

"That would give you some time to sharpen your skills and define your style."

Sherry hung her head. "My dad says I have to either find a *real* job, or he's going to kick me out of the house."

"That's harsh."

Rubbing her shoes together nervously, Sherry continued to stare down. "Dad's not known for his compassion. The Svenska Gotters are known for hard work and..."

"And what?"

Sherry looked up. "Intolerance of slackers."

"Your father would consider your career as an artist being a slacker?"

"It's not hard labor. He said he wants me to learn the value of sweat on my brow."

"He said, 'Sweat on your brow?'"

"Those were his words. He grew up on a farm and I think he wants me to milk cows and throw hay bales to appreciate the value of hard work." Sherry stared at me. "Did your father ever say things like that to you?"

"My father died when I was a teenager. My mother wasn't that involved in my life. She seemed happy that I pursued a degree in music."

"What did you do with your music degree? Is that what got you this job?"

I chuckled. "I joined the Navy and became a corpsman."

"Is a corpsman a musician?"

"Hardly. I trained to provide first aid for wounded Marines. I spent a year in Iraq before coming back to Two Harbors and finding this job."

"That's why Brian Johnson calls you Doc?"

"I prefer Peter to Doc."

"But that's why he calls you that? Because you were a corpsman?"

"Yes," I said, checking my watch, then glancing at the calendar of events. "I need to get moving. We've got a costume contest in a few minutes, and I need to tune my guitar and find Wendy."

Sherry cocked her head. "You need to tune your guitar for a costume contest?"

I lifted the guitar case from the corner behind my desk. "Wendy and I sing Halloween songs while the residents parade through in their costumes."

Sherry sighed. "I don't have any classes until this afternoon. Can I watch the costume contest?"

"Sure. Give me one second." I then removed my guitar from its case and strummed. Tuning the E string, I strummed it again, then stood. We walked together toward the activity room. "Actually, you can help. Some of the characters being represented aren't obvious. Stand by the door and ask each person who they're dressed as, then introduce them as they walk in."

"You can't tell who some of them are by their costumes?"

"No. Just ask them who they are and announce it to the room as they enter."

Sherry shrugged. "I can do that. What will you be doing?"

"Wendy and I will be singing Halloween songs."

"Are there many Halloween songs?" Sherry asked as we reached the activity room.

"There are dozens," I replied.

People were lined up outside the room. Looking at the number of residents who'd come in their daily clothing, I held the door open and announced, "If you're here to watch the costume contest, come in and take a seat. If you're in costume, please wait outside. Once everyone is seated, Wendy and I will start the songs. For those of you in costume, please tell my volunteer assistant, Sherry, who you are. She'll announce you as you march in."

A few dozen people walked past to take their seats. The people in costume let the others pass. Sherry took her place at the door just as Wendy arrived. "Start the music, Peter. I've got this."

Wendy walked with me to the front of the room. Leaning close, she asked, "Why is Sherry Vogel here?"

"Sherry showed up at my office this morning looking like she'd lost her last friend. I brought her along to introduce the costumed people."

Wendy shrugged. "Okay. Are we starting with 'Monster Mash'?"

"That sounds good." I picked the opening notes and started the song.

The first costumed residents at the door were Jeri and Lee Westfall. Lee was wearing a tux that looked like it had fit him a decade earlier, and Jeri wore a long dress. They whispered to Sherry, and she stepped into the room. "Nick and Nora Charles, *The Thin Man* and his wife, Nora."

The announcement brought on a round of chuckles, mostly because Lee was far from being thin, and the Nick Charles signature pencil-line mustache has been applied with an eyebrow pencil.

Next in line were Karla, Kathy, and Mary, in their lacy long dresses, recently borrowed from The Pine County History Museum. They whispered to Sherry who announced, "Anne Shirley, Diana Barry, and Marilla Cuthbert from *Anne of Green Gables*."

Their entrance was met with smiles and a few claps as they walked in, the three of them looking very proper and composed.

The next resident to be announced was Kurt Hegland, wearing a suit and bow tie. A *tastevin*, wine-sampling spoon hung from a silver chain around his neck. He whispered to Sherry who stepped forward as we ended the song. "The sommelier from *The Grand Hotel*."

The introduction brought chuckles and some clapping from the crowd. Wendy and I started singing Michael Jackson's "Thriller" as Kurt circled the room.

I could see a Stetson tipped down as someone wearing a buckskin vest whispered to Sherry. She nodded, then stepped into the room. "Annie Oakley," she announced. I groaned as Dolores my former neighbor who'd spent years shooting at the rabbits in her yard, walked into the room. I groaned again, seeing the vintage rifle she was carrying. Kerry and I had confiscated all of the guns we found in a search of her house. Dolores wasn't known for making sure her guns were unloaded before swinging them around. I watched closely to make sure the gun wasn't cocked, and her finger off the trigger as she walked around the room.

The parade of costumes continued through another song, then a last resident showed up wearing a fur coat. I was more focused on the chords of the Michael Jackson song than I was on the costume, but my head jerked up when Sherry announced, "Ava Gardner."

Alma Kotter walked forward, wrapped in a mink coat. Knowing that Ava Gardner was well known for exposing herself to Frank Sinatra by opening her fur coat while naked, I froze in mid-strum. "No!" I yelled as Alma strutted forward.

Unaware of the issue, Sherry shook her head at me and gestured that she didn't understand my outburst. I handed my guitar to Wendy and rushed to Alma, who was completely into her Ava Gardner persona and was nearing the front of the room. Many residents had seen Ava Gardner open her coat, exposing herself during a boat cruise during the town's recent pirate festival. Many of the women frowned with disgust. A few of the men stood to get a better view of Alma's upcoming revelation. Most of the crowd was unaware of what was about to happen.

I reached Alma, stepped behind her, then wrapped my arms around her in a bear hug, a moment before she threw open her coat. "Peter!" She said in a way that sounded provocative. "I didn't know you cared!"

The crowd laughed. I leaned next to Alma's ear. "We're going for less exposure. Keep your coat closed."

Batting her glued-on eyelashes, she replied, "I thought I'd give the boys a thrill, like Ava did for Frank."

"Not today."

"I bet that would get the most votes for best costume."

"Keep your mink closed," I whispered. "Let everyone's imagination fill in the rest of your performance."

Sherry arrived at my side. "What's going on?"

"Alma is naked under her coat. She's planning on flashing the crowd once I let go of her. Grab a tablecloth, sheet, or coat to cover her."

Sherry removed a white plastic tablecloth from a nearby table and wrapped it around Ava.

"Thank you," I said.

Alma pouted. "Party poopers."

Trying to recover from the near disrobing, I gestured for the costumed residents to line up across the front of the room. "Please clap for your favorite costume when I hold my hand over the characters."

I walked behind the people, holding my hand over each costumed person, and listened to the applause. When I reached Dolores, I carefully took the gun from her.

"Where did you find another gun?" I whispered.

"My nephew died, and his widow brought this rifle to me. My husband had loaned it to him when he was a boy with the stipulation that he return it to us. She found a note with it when she cleared out his hunting gear and she returned it to me last week." Smiling, she added, "Don't you think it was a nice touch for my costume?"

"It was perfect. I'll take care of it for you." I made sure it wasn't loaded, then set it in a corner.

The applause was polite for everyone until I got to the end of the row and raised my hands over Nick and Nora Charles. The applause increased and someone whistled from the back of the audience.

"It appears that the winners of this year's costume contest are Lee and Jeri Westfall, dressed as Nick and Nora Charles!"

Sherry helped Wendy and I rearrange the chairs as the residents filed out of the room. "Was that woman really going to flash the crowd?"

Wendy laughed. "Alma has flashed people in the past. I assume she was willing to bare it all again." She paused and looked at Sherry. "That shouldn't be shocking. You posed nude for an art class."

"That was different. What I did was artistic, for a group of people learning to draw the human body. This would've been...I don't know, tasteless, maybe."

Nodding my agreement, I straightened the last chair in the row, then retrieved Dolores' gun from the corner. "I agree." Looking at Wendy, I said, "Some people are just into exposing themselves."

Wendy laughed and touched Sherry's shoulder. "Peter is just upset because I've shown people my tattoos. Some of them are in somewhat private locations."

Sherry blushed. "I think that would be embarrassing."

Laughing, Wendy said, "Some of us are more uninhibited than others."

I gestured toward the door, then locked the room behind us. Sherry followed me to my office where I hid the rifle behind the door and said, "Your job is really cool. What else do you do?"

"I drive people to the mall to go shopping. I show a weekly movie. I try to find seasonally appropriate activities that the residents enjoy."

"What degree would I need to get a job like yours?"

"I don't know. I have a music degree, but I'm sure there are specific degrees in recreation and entertainment that would fit."

Stopping outside my office, Sherry paused. "You're really interesting and fun. Thanks for letting me follow you around this morning."

"You're welcome to join me anytime. The residents seemed to enjoy seeing a young, new face."

"I'm going to talk to my advisor when I get back on campus. Maybe there are some classes I could take this spring that would qualify me for a job like yours."

"That sounds like a plan."

I watched Sherry walk away. She had a spring in her step that hadn't been there when she arrived. Brian Johnson surprised me when he said, "Why don't witches wear flat hats?"

"I don't know."

"There's no point in it."

I groaned but grabbed a pencil and notepad to record the joke for Jeremy.

"You didn't tell Sherry that recreation directors made only slightly more than unemployed artists and musicians."

I sighed. "I didn't want to burst her bubble."

"You aren't going to leave the gun behind your door, are you?"

I blew out a breath. "I'll put it in my gun safe with the rest of Dolores' arsenal."

Brian chuckled. "I'd take it off your hands, but there's really no way to carry a tuba and a rifle."

“You haven’t told me a tuba Halloween joke.”

Shaking his head, Brian sighed. “I’ve searched for one. I’ve got Christmas, Hanukkah, and Lent, but nothing with a tuba and Halloween.”

“You must be devastated.”

A cherubic smile appeared on Brian’s face. “Did you hear about the tubist and bass player who broke up?” He paused a beat. “The relationship ended on a low blow.”

I grimaced as he walked away.

Chapter 14

The Halloween weather forecast predicted unseasonably mild temperatures. There had been frost overnight, but the trick-or-treating outlook was for the temperature to hover in the 40s. Unlike some years, when the children wore their costumes over snowmobile suits, tonight they would only need jackets, gloves, and stocking caps.

Jeremy raced down for breakfast with energy usually reserved for evenings. "Dad, can I go trick-or-treating with the Stones? The people in their neighborhood give out way better candy than the people around here," he said as he pulled a box of cereal out of the cupboard.

"Is this about better candy, or about being able to get into more trouble with Jacob than you will with your mom and Amy?"

Jeremy took a bowl from the cupboard and spoon from the drawer. "Do you really think Mrs. Stone would let us get into trouble?"

"Will Mrs. Stone be walking with you?"

The pause before Jeremy's answer was suspicious. "I think we'll be going with their neighbors. Mrs. Stone has to stay home to hand out candy because Chief Stone is going to do cop stuff all night."

Certain that Deb Stone wouldn't let Jacob do anything terribly stupid or risky, I felt at ease letting Jeremy go with Jacob. "Sure, but you have to promise me you won't get into trouble or eat more than four candy bars. Okay?"

"Sure," Jeremy replied as he poured milk on his cereal. I was fairly certain that he'd either not heard or planned to ignore whatever I'd said.

"I have to be in town all day for the festival. Will you help your mother with Amy while I'm gone?"

"Dad..."

"Yes, or no?"

Jeremy looked at me over his spoon. "I suppose you'll go all professor on me if I say no."

"Good guess."

"Fine."

Hearing Jenny on the stairs, I poured a second mug of coffee for her and set it on the table. She kissed me as she passed by, then she buckled Amy into the highchair. "When do you need to be in town?"

"Now."

She looked up as she strapped Amy in. "You'll be okay, right?"

"I don't expect any problems."

"You never expect problems."

"Face it, you're married to an optimist."

Jenny walked to me and wrapped her arms around my neck. "An optimist, or the most naïve man in Two Harbors."

"Maybe some of both."

* * *

I parked near the 3M museum, assuming that would be away from the crowds, and would make for an easier exit after the festivities. Passing the art studio, I saw the owner staring through the window, her hands wrapped around a coffee mug. Based on experience with her, I suspected the coffee mug was full of brown liquor even though it wasn't yet noon.

I stepped through the door and smiled. "Are you expecting a crowd today?"

She leaned her hip against a table supporting a marble sculpture. "What I expect and what happens are often two very different things."

"Plan for the worst and hope for the best," I replied.

"I heard my favorite nude model judged the pumpkin pie competition with you."

"I think Sherry's father offered her judging services as penance for her stint as your nude model."

"Yeah, I knew her holy-roller father would have a problem with Sherry posing in the nude. But she has a really cute body." Melissa's grin was unnerving. "Don't you agree?"

"I didn't notice."

162

"You're a terrible liar, Peter. Your face is bright red."

"I stared into Sherry's eyes the entire time."

Melissa chuckled. "Yeah, you Navy veterans are well known for your lack of peripheral vision."

I wished Melissa good sales and walked toward the park. Brian Johnson, the tuba expert, and the football coach were marking three-foot by three-foot squares, using the machine normally used for making the yardage lines on the football field. They'd strung crime scene tape around the area to keep people from walking on the grid and were using string as a guide for making the lines.

Brian looked up when they completed one line. "Remind me why I'm helping with this?" he asked.

"What else would you be doing?"

"Let's see, I could be drinking coffee while completing a crossword puzzle, practicing my tuba, or...anything where I'd be inside and warm."

"This is a public service, Brian."

"That's what they tell convicts who pick up trash from the ditches, right?"

"What's the band planning to play during the alpaca bingo?"

Brian smiled. "The director found music for 'Donkey Serenade'. It seems fitting."

* * *

The aroma of hot Booya filled the chilly air in Owens Park. People sat at all the available picnic tables, happily slurping Booya from plastic spoons supplied by the firemen serving the Styrofoam bowls of the stew-like Booya. I marveled at the thirty people in line, each with a five-dollar bill in hand.

Stepping behind Sparky, who was collecting the money from people approaching the boiling cauldron. "It looks like you won't be able to have a Booya feed for too many more years."

"What do you mean?" Sparky asked over his shoulder.

"Everyone in line has gray hair. Your Booya audience is dying out."

Sparky looked down the line of customers, assessing their age. "I think some are buying Booya for their children and grandchildren. You've got to get them hooked when they're young."

"I think it's like the Sons of Norway lutefisk feed. If you aren't forced to eat it as a child, it's something that you never develop a taste for."

Chuckling, Sparky nodded. "I suppose we'll get to that point in the future. In the meanwhile, we'll still make Booya, and all the hunters and fishermen will be able to clean out the freezer-burned meat from the previous season."

"Gee, Sparky. Your marketing pitch leaves something to be desired. 'Have some of our Booya so the hunters can clear out their freezer-burned venison.' It makes my mouth water."

Putting his hand on a stack of money so it wouldn't blow away or be stolen, Sparky turned to me. "Stop that. People like Booya because it's a hearty soup made with a secret blend of herbs and spices."

"Mmm. Wonderful herbs and spices that cover the flavor of the freezer-burned meat."

Walter Hagen listened to our conversation as he scooped Booya from the cauldron and ladled it into bowls for the people in line. "You two need to shut your pie holes before you chase off the customers," he said.

"Pie holes?" I asked.

Walter frowned at me. "Didn't your mother ever call your mouth a pie hole?"

"Nope, she always told me to shut my mouth."

"Well, pie hole is your new phrase for the day. Now, get out of here. You're ruining the ambiance of the Booya experience."

I looked at the line of people dressed in cool weather gear, some shivering, others blowing into their clasped hands to keep them warm. Beyond them were the people eating, bent over bowls of Booya, hoping to warm themselves by slurping up the warm stew. "Walt, I don't think ambiance is the correct word for this...situation."

Sparky glanced around, then realized everyone nearby would hear whatever he was about to say. Trying to be obtuse, he said, "Is the covert operation still on for tonight?"

I searched my memory for anything that would be considered a covert operation. Coming up blank I asked, "What covert operation?"

"Kerry said he would talk to you about it."

"He hasn't mentioned anything to me. If it involves anything other than tucking the kids into bed, I'm going to pass."

Sparky cocked his head. "You're a key member of the arson investigation team. I'm sure we need you for Kerry's plan."

I waved my hand dismissively. "I'm sure the investigation can proceed without me. Right now, I have to shop for pumpkin bowling and Jack-o-lantern painting supplies."

"You mean pumpkin carving, don't you?"

"Think about it, Sparky. Would you give a few dozen senior citizens with shaking hands sharp knives to carve pumpkins?"

Without hesitation, Sparky shook his head. "Um, no. That painting plan sounds much better."

A woman's voice hailed me as I walked away from the park. "Peter!"

Sherry Vogel waved her arm as she jogged toward me. "What's up, Sherry?"

"Meg Cochran told me to help you today. What are you doing?"

"Right now, I'm going to the grocery store, then I'll be supervising pumpkin bowling and jack-o-lantern painting."

"Meg mentioned alpaca bingo."

"That's this afternoon. This morning, I've got to put on my Whistling Pines recreation director hat and coordinate senior citizens' activities."

Sherry looked around the park. Spotting someone or something, she froze. "Can I help with your pumpkin activities?"

"You don't need to."

Breaking eye contact with whomever had caused her to tense up, Sherry looked at me. "I need to help you *all day*. It's part of my commitment to the Halloween festival."

"My Whistling Pines activities have nothing to do with..."

Sherry stopped me. "Please, Peter. I need you to keep me busy today."

The tension in Sherry's voice made me look in the direction she'd been staring. Across the park, one of the Svenska Gotter members was glaring at us. "Do you need to get away from the members of your father's congregation?"

Nodding, she replied, "Please..."

"You're welcome to accompany me on whatever errands I have to make and to assist with the activities at Whistling Pines. You were a big help with the costume contest. That said, I can't be the long-term escape strategy for avoiding your father's church congregation. You need something more permanent."

Sherry nodded as she relaxed and looked less like she was going to run away. "Thank you, Peter. I'm focused on today. I'll come up with something else for tomorrow. Maybe Meg needs help in her shop."

I felt sorry for Sherry as she followed me to my car like a lost puppy. *I can't save her from her parents and the Svenska Gotters*, I thought, while feeling guilty for not having an exit plan for her in my pocket.

* * *

My grocery stop was simple. I loaded ten two-liter bottles of the cheapest brand of soda pop available while Sherry held the shopping cart. "Peter, I think you'd better buy a couple spare bottles, in case one breaks."

Weighing the wisdom of Sherry's suggestion, I added four more bottles of the bargain soda to the cart. As we pushed the cart away from the soda pop section, I turned toward the paper products.

"What do you need down here?" Sherry asked.

"You pointed out the potential problem with using soda bottles as bowling pins. If one breaks, we'll have a mess to clean up." I added a four-pack of paper towels and a package of wet wipes, placing them alongside the soda bottles in our shopping cart.

"What else do we need?" Sherry asked as I pushed the cart toward the cash registers.

"There's a pumpkin farmer who offered to donate misshapen pumpkins for my jack-o-lantern painting. We'll stop at his farm next."

"You'll need a few bowling ball sized pumpkins too."

After loading the soda pop into my car, we drove south out of town to the pumpkin farm. Kyle Peterson had a stand set up next to his driveway next to an array of prime pumpkins arranged on rough shelves he'd made from a variety of lumber. The stand was empty, a hand-painted sign asked anyone taking a pumpkin to leave two dollars in a plastic coffee can sitting on the counter.

Sherry eyed the sign and coffee can. "I don't think this would work in Duluth. Someone would take the pumpkins and the money."

"I'm not convinced that won't happen here, too. I suppose it's boring to sit in this stand all day waiting for someone to buy a pumpkin."

"I'd love that. I could read a book or cruise the internet in silence all day long."

"Maybe that can be your plan for tomorrow."

Sherry giggled. "Meg said you were clueless about a lot of things."

"What am I clueless about?"

"Tomorrow is All Saints Day, the day after Halloween. The cost of pumpkins will drop to zero. No one buys a pumpkin after Halloween."

"Sure. I knew that." I looked toward the house, but not seeing even a vehicle, I decided to take the farmer at his word. "Let's pick some pumpkins out of the field. I assume anything that's left there is surplus."

To Sherry's credit, she rushed to the field and began carrying back two pumpkins at a time. As directed, she found the ugliest, misshapen pumpkins I'd ever seen. Within a few minutes we'd filled my trunk and back seat with pumpkins. In her last load, Sherry carried four smaller pumpkins, close to the size of bowling balls. "I think these will work for pumpkin bowling. They've all got stems for people to grab, and they're not too heavy."

My car quickly filled with an earthy, pumpkin aroma as we drove back to Two Harbors. Despite having dirty hands from the pumpkins, Sherry seemed content with our mission. "You know, if any guy my age had driven me out of town to pick up free pumpkins, I'd probably have jumped from the car before we left town."

"Really?"

"Guys are jerks with only one thing on their minds."

I smiled at her. "Pizza?"

Snorting, she said, "Okay, two things on their minds. But the pizza definitely comes after the first one."

"They outgrow that stage."

"When they're like fifty?" she asked.

"There are jerks regardless of their age. Most guys outgrow that. We want love and companionship when we're mature."

Sherry considered that on the rest of our drive to Whistling Pines.

Chapter 15

We unloaded pumpkins and soda pop from my car, transferring them into a shopping cart stored in the entryway. It took three trips to bring everything into the activities room.

"Now we set up tables and chairs."

"What are you going to use to paint the jack-o-lanterns?"

"I have colored pens in the closet. I think that's our best bet for a low mess coloring option."

Sherry was setting out the pens as the first residents arrived. After giving a few directions, she dove into getting pumpkins for people, then helping them draw eyes, noses, and teeth. The residents loved her enthusiasm, and Sherry had an amazing ability to deal with their grumbling, disabilities, and gnarled fingers. Until Hulda Packer arrived.

Pushing her walker like a snow plow, Hulda banged into the table nearest the door, then crunched a series of occupied chairs. "Peter, why didn't you save me a seat near the door? You know that I can't walk long distances."

Sherry brought a folding chair from the corner and set it up at the end of the nearest table. "Sherry, this is Mrs. Packer. She will probably need some help."

"Help?" Hulda snapped. "I'm perfectly capable of doing things for myself." She paused. "What *are* we doing?"

Sherry held out an array of colored pens. "We're making jack-o-lanterns, Mrs. Packer. What color would you like first?"

"Why do I need a pen? Where's my knife? I need a knife to carve a jack-o-lantern."

Seeing Sherry's look of concern, I rushed over. "We're using colored pens because they allows a greater degree of creativity than simply carving the pumpkins." I pointed toward Mary, Karla, and Kathy, my three relatively sane artists. "Look at the lovely designs some of the other people are creating."

"Anyone can color on a pumpkin. It takes *skill* to carve a jack-o-lantern. Besides, where will we put the candles if we don't cut open the tops?"

Karla came to my rescue. "Isn't it time to start the pumpkin bowling, Peter?"

Making a show of checking my watch, I nodded. "Yes, it is! Let's clear the side of the room where we'll be setting up a bowling alley."

Sherry took the cue and pushed the shopping cart with the soda pop bottles to the far side of the room. "I'll set up the pins."

"Hulda, would you like to bowl first?"

"What do I win?"

Having no plans for prizes, I paused. "I suppose anyone who gets a strike will get a certificate."

Hulda gave me her best *stink eye* look. "A certificate. That's the best you've got?"

Wendy arrived with my guitar, which gave us a moment of distraction from the certificate discussion. "We're going to sing bowling songs," she announced.

"Bowling songs?" I mouthed.

Wendy nodded. "The bowling song from the movie *Grease 2*. You know it. 'We're Going to Score Tonight'."

It took a second for me to flash back to the ridiculous bowling alley scene from the movie. Quickly replaying the song in my head, I visualized the chord sequence and strummed them. Nodding to Wendy, she sang the opening line, "Come on everybody, gather 'round. I'm going to show you how to knock 'em down..."

Sherry waved Kathy Christensen over to our makeshift bowling lane and handed her one of the smaller pumpkins. Looking like a pro bowler lining up her shot, Kathy swung the pumpkin as she took two steps, then let it slide across the floor.

Sherry rushed down the room, quickly resetting the two soda bottles that Kathy's shot had knocked down.

I gestured toward the reset pins and called out, "I'm sure someone can do better than that! Who's next?"

Mary smiled and took a slightly larger pumpkin from the table. Showing less technique than Kathy, but putting more oomph into her shot, Mary's pumpkin hit the head pin squarely, bouncing it off the soda bottles behind, and knocking down seven of them.

Karla stepped up as Sherry reset the bottles. "In the day, I had a bowling league leading two-hundred average." With good bowling form, Karla raised her pumpkin in two hands, aiming it at the pop bottles. Stepping forward, she swung the pumpkin back and released it as it touched the floor.

Wendy went on, singing "We're going to score tonight..."

Hearing the double entendre, I frowned. Wendy smiled and nodded toward the residents who were tapping their toes and focusing on Karla's shot. The pumpkin was sliding toward the strike pocket, just to the right of the head pin/bottle. The perfect shot was ruined when the pumpkin's stem flipped around causing the pumpkin to veer to the left, missing all the soda bottles. The miss caused the residents to groan in mock disappointment. Karla put on a fake pout and demanded a reload with a different pumpkin.

Ending the bowling song, I looked at Wendy for the title of another song. "'Beer Frame Judy'," she said.

I had to dig deep into my memory to recall the song, played by The Front 4. I played the long guitar intro as Ginny Johnson selected a pumpkin. Ginny was lining up her shot as Wendy sang the opening line. Ginny lacked technique and strength, causing the pumpkin to slowly roll down the room as Wendy sang the chorus, "Beer frame Judy, pour us another round..."

Ginny's shot hit the headpin/bottle causing it to totter, but not fall. The room laughed as people clapped to the music. Ginny shook her head, then stepped aside when Hulda's walker bumped into her legs.

"Move aside," Hulda ordered, selecting a pumpkin she was barely able to lift with one hand. Pushing her walker aside, Hulda pushed the pumpkin with two hands, as if making a basketball free throw. It flew three feet, then fell to the floor with a thud. The impact causing it to crack open.

Sherry raced to the pumpkin and picked it up. "Too bad. You got a defective pumpkin. Try again."

Giving Sherry the stink eye, Hulda grabbed her walker. "This game is rigged." She spun the walker around, hitting Joe Wakeman in the shin, then banging into me. Ignoring my efforts to play guitar and keep the beat, she snarled at me. "This is a stupid game. Let's do turkey bowling next time. I won a turkey at the grocery store last Thanksgiving."

Wendy shrugged off Hulda's comments and whispered, "'Let's go Bowling' by the Arrogant Worms."

"Some of the lyrics are a bit offensive."

Wendy looked at the crowd. "No one is listening to the words. Play."

I played the opening guitar riff and Wendy sang the opening words, "Grab your balls and shoes..."

Sherry continued to encourage the bowlers and set up the pins they knocked down. Wendy sang. I came up with the chords for more and more obscure bowling songs, including "Bowling Alley Thug" and "Bowling Ball Blues".

The event ended when Lee Westfall got a strike that broke open two soda bottles, spraying sticky soda pop all over Sherry, the walls, and the floor.

I ended "Bowling Trophy Wife" and set my guitar aside, safely away from the splattered soda pop. "I think Lee wins the grand prize."

Puffing up, Lee smiled and bowed to the crowd. I took a paper certificate from a folder and wrote Lee's name on it with a Sharpie pen. He accepted the Championship Bowler Certificate as if I'd just presented him with a check for a million dollars.

The crowd filtered out of the room as Sherry wiped soda pop off her face, hair, and sweatshirt with paper towels while Wendy put the unbroken bottles and pumpkins back into the shopping cart. Having been watching from the back of the room, Bingle, our maintenance man, disappeared, then showed up pushing a mop cart and mop.

Sherry's face was flushed with excitement. "This was fun. Do you get to do things like this every day?"

"There's always something," I replied.

Overhearing the conversation as she pushed the shopping cart to the door, Wendy stopped next to us. "Have you ever considered giving up your modeling gigs and considering a career in geriatric recreation, Sherry?"

"Geriatric recreation?" Sherry asked.

"Entertaining old people," Wendy explained. "There are thousands of senior residences being built every year. Each of them needs someone enthusiastic and fun to organize and execute the recreation activities."

Sherry looked at me. "Is that a *thing*?"

"I doubt there's a degree program in geriatric recreation, but there are hundreds of recreation directors in senior facilities who are arranging and coordinating programs."

"Where do you get your program ideas? Is there like a book of programs or an internet site with suggestions?"

Wendy laughed. "Peter flies by the seat of his pants. There are seasonal programs, and weekly events, like movies, but the residents love when Peter dreams up something different, something that breaks up the monotony of life."

"The people really seemed to enjoy your music," Sherry said to Wendy.

"Do you play an instrument?"

Sherry nodded and looked at me. "I play clarinet. Peter has been giving me lessons to sharpen my skills. I'd like to learn how to play the guitar."

"Can you sing?"

"I was in the high school and church choirs, but I've never sung a solo."

Wendy nodded toward the door. "Come on. Peter, grab your guitar."

Pushing the shopping cart, Wendy led us to the atrium, near the bird aviary. She led Sherry to a spot under the mounted moose head. "What songs do you know?" She whispered.

Embarrassed, Sherry shrugged. "Um, I can't sing a solo in front of a bunch of people."

Wendy leaned close to Sherry's ear. "You're brave. You can do this. It's less embarrassing than posing for an art class. Name a song."

"'Over the Rainbow'."

Wendy nodded to me, and I strummed the opening chords, then hummed the opening, waiting for Sherry. "Somewhere, over the rainbow, way up high..."

Wendy sang harmony with the second verse, surprising Sherry. With a smile, Wendy urged her on through the third verse and the ending. The residents gathered during the song, clapping when it ended.

"Another," Wendy whispered.

Sherry looked confused. "What?"

"Name another song you know."

"'The Lion Sleeps Tonight'."

Wendy nodded to me. "You've got the falsetto, Peter."

I sang the opening "Wimoweh..."

Sherry waited for the lyrical opening and sang. "In the jungle..."

More residents gathered as Sherry sang the refrain, with Wendy and me singing the harmony and nonsense words in the background. During the second verse, Nancy walked out of her office and stood listening in the hallway, with her arms crossed.

As the applause died, Wendy gestured to Sherry and addressed the audience. "Thank you. Our guest vocalist today is Sherry Vogel."

Wendy led Sherry through the crowd with me wondering what she was going to do next. Pushing Sherry in front of Nancy, she said, "Nancy, this is Sherry Vogel. She'd like to be our recreation intern."

Nancy raised her eyebrows and glanced at me. "We've never had an intern before. What would she do?"

Wendy smiled. "She's great with the residents and has a lovely voice. I think she would add enthusiasm to our programs and music."

Nancy smiled at Sherry, then looked at me. "How's your recreation budget?"

Being unprepared for the whole discussion, I shrugged. "I think it's in good shape."

"Can you afford a part-time intern?"

Sherry's hopeful look was disarming. "No problem. We'll have to talk about salary and hours. Sherry's still a UMD student, and we'll have to work around her class schedule."

Nancy nodded. "Can you work weekends, Sherry?"

"Yes! And Tuesday and Thursday evenings."

Nancy smiled. "Peter, it looks like you can start taking Saturdays off once you get Sherry trained. Do you have a spare set of keys she can have?"

"I'm sure there's a set in my desk," I replied. "We'll have to do a background check, and she'll have to fill out a W-4."

Cocking her head, Nancy smiled at Sherry. "I think we can forgo the background check. We know Sherry and her background." Extending her hand, Nancy said, "Welcome to Whistling Pines, Sherry. I hope you don't mind sharing an office with Wendy."

"I get an office?"

Wendy frowned. "It's more like a desk in the corner."

"Cool! I've never had a real job before. My dad..."

"Your dad?" I asked.

"I think he'll be okay with this. It's not like I'll be working as a waitress or modeling."

Nancy ran her tongue around the inside of her mouth while staring at me. "I can assure you that modeling is not part of your job description. Right, Peter?"

"Right, no modeling involved."

Wendy's Cheshire Cat grin appeared. "Yeah, I'm the only one modeling for the art classes."

Nancy slid her glasses down, looking at Wendy over the top rim. "Your modeling career is over, too. Are we clear on that?"

"But..."

"It's over, Wendy. Covered by the morality clause in your contract."

Wendy sighed. "But I can still play in the band."

"The band is fine as long as your lyrics and antics don't reflect poorly on Whistling Pines," Nancy replied.

Chapter 16

Jenny joined me in the atrium as Sherry returned the guitar to my office. "Guess who has a new intern?"

Jenny's confusion was written on her face. "What are you talking about?"

"Wendy suggested a candidate to be the recreation director's intern and Nancy agreed."

Jenny grinned. "I didn't know you were searching for an intern."

"I wasn't, but a candidate with impeccable credentials showed up."

"Is it someone from town?"

"Sort of. She's a UMD student."

"What are you planning to have her do?"

I smiled and said, "Nancy said I can take weekends off."

"That's great. It means Whistling Pines will have someone doing recreation activities seven days a week without you working almost every one of your days off."

"I'm looking forward to it."

"You still haven't told me if it's someone I know."

"It's Sherry Vogel."

"Sherry, the minister's daughter and nude model?"

"That's her."

"What qualifications does she have beyond modeling?"

"About the same set I brought to this job. She's an art student who's good with our residents. She's polite, energetic, and she can sing."

"Are you planning for her to start in-house art classes?"

"That's a thought. She's an art major. She'll bring a different skillset to the job."

"I'm a little concerned about who will be modeling for those art classes."

Feeling stupid for not catching the implications of the question, I quickly explained that Nancy had specifically said there would be no nude modeling by anyone, including Wendy.

"Okay, then. You're now a supervisor in addition to your other duties. You'll have to make sure she's well directed and busy." Jenny paused. "And be aware that doing crossword puzzles in the dining room is not acceptable behavior."

"Wendy claims the crossword puzzles give her a chance to keep an eye on the residents."

"It's more like it gives her time to stir up things that don't need agitation."

"Like the calendar project," Jenny said as Sherry returned.

Sherry cocked her head. "Who made a calendar?"

Bingle, who was carrying a ladder past, overheard us. He chuckled and replied in his thick Swedish accent, "Oh, yah. Last year, the ladies had their naked photos made into calendar pages. It's the best fundraiser we've ever had."

Grimacing as visions of our naked residents flashed through her mind, Sherry asked, "The residents had their pictures taken naked?'

Jenny clarified, "To be accurate, the women were discreetly covered, but there was a lot of sagging skin showing."

Sherry looked to Jenny. "How did their families react?"

Jenny wrinkled her nose. "I had the impression their adult children thought it was tasteful. I'm sure some of their grandchildren were surprised to see grandma standing naked behind a flower vase."

Overwhelmed by the visions of some of the more *voluptuous* residents, Sherry asked, "Were flower vases large enough?"

Bingle shook his head. "In some cases, vases weren't big enough. One woman had to stand behind a hedge...for adequate coverage."

"A hedge?" Sherry asked.

"That, among other props." Bingle was ready to expand when I cut him off.

"Is the activity room floor dry, or do we need to put up a sign to warn people?"

Bingle nodded toward the room. "I locked the door to make sure no one slips and falls."

"Thank you."

Bingle stepped away and Jenny cocked her head. "Why is the activity room floor wet?"

"A bottle of soda pop exploded during pumpkin bowling."

Jenny shook her head, then flicked her fingers at me. "Just go. You can explain it to me later."

"It's really not a big deal. Lee Westfall got a strike after Hulda got mad and left."

Jenny glanced at my watch. "Don't you need to be in the dining room. I saw people gathering for the Halloween word game."

Turning to Sherry I said, "There is a stack of A-to-Z word game sheets on top of my printer. Would you retrieve them while I get pencils from the stockroom?"

"Sure!" Sherry said before rushing off.

Jenny looked at me. "I wish my staff were that enthusiastic."

"I wish I had Sherry's energy," I replied as we walked toward the stock room.

* * *

Two dozen residents were gathered in the dining room when I arrived with a box of pencils. Most were having conversations with the people at their tables. Hulda sat alone near the door. "It's about time you got here," she grumbled.

Smiling, I moved among the tables handing out pencils. "Our game is a Halloween themed word search. You'll each get a sheet of paper with the letters A to Z. The goal is to write in one word associated with Halloween that starts with each letter. You don't have to do the words in order, just fill in as many words as you can. I'll set a timer for five minutes. At the end of the time, everyone will stop writing and you'll count the number of words you've written down. The person who's remembered the most words, wins."

I was about to tell Sherry to hand out the sheets when Karla raised her hand. "Who is going to check the words? What if someone writes down a word that has nothing to do with Halloween?"

"Don't you think everyone can be on their honor?" I asked.

There was a chorus of, "NO," responses.

I looked at Karla, Mary, and Kathy, who were often the more objective participants in my games. "How do we deal with this?"

"It's easy," said Karla. "Have everyone pass their sheet to the person next to them for scoring. If there are any questionable answers, you can be the arbitrator."

Nodding, I gestured for Sherry to pass out the sheets. "Everyone keep your sheet face down until all the forms are handed out. When I say, 'go," you flip them over. I'll start the timer and after five minutes I'll stop the game. Then, you'll pass your sheet to the person next to you."

Sherry nodded to me as she set the last game sheets in front of Jeri and Lee Westfall who were sitting in the back of the room.

"Go!"

Sherry threaded her way among the tables as she returned to the front of the dining room. "Does it bother you that some people are peeking at others' answers?"

"It's not school, there's no cash prize, and I don't want to be the game police. So, no, I don't care."

Sherry looked at me with wonder. "I love this place. Everything is so laid back and everyone seems to be having fun."

"In sixty years, you can move in."

Hulda, sitting nearest to us, glanced up. "Shh. I'm trying to concentrate."

The writing slowed at the three-minute mark. After five minutes, Karla was the only person who seemed to be writing anything down.

"Time's up! Pass your paper clockwise."

Hulda glared at me. "Which way is the clock facing?"

"What do you mean, Hulda?"

"Clockwise goes opposite directions depending on which wrist you're wearing your watch on."

Rather than arguing or explaining, I said, "Pass your paper to the left."

The scoring went quickly, and most papers had been counted in less than a minute. The exception was Ginny Johnson, who appeared to struggle with Hulda's answers. I knelt next to her. "Is there a problem?"

"Aside from not being able to read Hulda's handwriting, I can't accept some of these as Halloween words."

"Give me an example," I said.

Ginny stood, with Hulda glaring at her. "Does anyone think 'Quaker' is a Halloween word?"

"Hang on!" Hulda said, struggling to stand. "Quakers were the ones who burned witches on Halloween. Everyone knows that!"

Sherry giggled, then looked at me to see how I'd react. Not wanting to be the arbitrator, I nodded. "Let's have a show of hands. Anyone who thinks we should accept Quaker as a Halloween word, raise your hand."

No hands went up. Then Hulda started giving people at nearby tables the stink eye. One by one, their hands went up.

Mary Gilbert stood, then stepped away from her table. "I abstain."

"Why?" I asked.

"I don't want my grandchildren to develop warts like the last time Hulda gave me the stink eye."

Sherry leaned close. "Is this for real?"

I nodded. "Fine. Sherry and I have decided that Quaker is *not* a Halloween word. Are there any other words to consider?"

Ginny adjusted her reading glasses. "How about Zoomba? Is that a Halloween word?"

I looked at Hulda. "What's a Zoomba?"

"Those are the exercise pants women wear to the gym."

Baffled by the word and Hulda's answer I asked, "What does that have to do with Halloween?"

After snorting derisively, Hulda said, "People wear them to the gym on Halloween."

I looked at Sherry, who was getting Hulda's stink eye glare. "What do you think?"

"I don't want warts. I refuse to vote."

"No one is getting warts."

"That blonde woman said her grandchildren got warts after Hulda gave her the stink eye."

I turned to Ginny. "How many Halloween words does Hulda have?"

"Two. Quaker and Zoomba."

Feeling a weight lifted from my shoulders, I addressed the room. "Does anyone have more than two words?" Dozens of hands went up. "What's the highest count?"

People shouted out eleven, then fourteen. The last person to answer was Kathy Christensen. "Karla has twenty-one."

I looked around the room. "Does anyone have more than twenty-one words?" Not getting a response, I announced, "Then, Karla is our winner!"

Sherry tapped me on the shoulder and gestured toward her wrist, like I should check the time. "Don't we need to see Meg about alpacas?"

"Right. Let's go."

* * *

"They're so cute!" Sherry said as Brandi lowered the tailgate. Sherry reached in and patted the neck of the nearest alpaca. The animal responded to her touch by tipping its head and pressing its ear into her hand.

Brandi watched. "They make great pets. They're very trainable and clean. Their wool is hypoallergenic."

"They're so soft," Sherry said as the alpaca continued to respond to her touch. "He likes me."

Brandi led the other alpaca out of the trailer by its colorful halter. "They like most people, although they're rather distrustful of crowds." She looked at me. "And men."

As if on cue, the animal Brandi was leading spit at me. It kept a careful eye on me as she tied it to a rail mounted on the trailer's side. She took the other alpaca's halter and led it down the ramp past my helper.

"By the way, my name is Brandi," the alpaca owner said.

"I'm Sherry Vogel."

"You've been petting Donner."

"Are all your animals named after Santa's reindeer?"

"I ran out of reindeer when the eighth one was born. I'm working my way through the seven dwarfs now. The second animal is named Doc."

"Is there any significance to the name Doc?" I asked.

Brandi chuckled. "He was a difficult delivery, and the vet bill was substantial. I threatened to give him to the vet in lieu of payment."

"The vet declined?" I asked.

"He's actually ten times more valuable than the vet fee."

Both alpacas took to Sherry, who was reveling in their nuzzling and rubbing. A crowd started to gather, Brandi and Sherry managed the crowd so only one person at a time interacted with the animals. Brandi answered questions and stopped people who tried to feed the animals. She explained that they got sick if they were fed flowers or vegetable pieces that were too big. When the crowd started pressing too close, Brandi, Sherry and I backed them away.

"Sherry, would you like to help me walk Doc and Donner around the squares for the bingo game?" Brandi asked.

"Really? You're not going to just let them wander randomly?" I asked.

"They're shy and would probably just stand in the middle of the square if we didn't lead them around. They don't like crowds." Brandi looked at me. "I was planning to ask Peter if he'd help, but they obviously like you better than Peter."

"What do I have to do?" Sherry asked.

"Lead Doc around the marked off area so that he walks through every square. I'll do the same with Donner. You go back and forth. I'll go end to end."

"Got it."

The musicians were tuning their instruments in the bandstand when Meg took the microphone. "Okay folks, we'll start alpaca bingo in five minutes. Volunteers wearing bright green vests will be selling bingo squares until the music begins, signaling the start of the game. All proceeds from the bingo square sales go to the Friends of the Bandshell. The game ends when the second alpaca...makes a deposit in one of the squares."

Brandi handed Doc's halter to Sherry and turned toward me. "Will you open the yellow barrier for us, Peter?"

I untied the crime scene tape letting the two alpacas and their handlers into the square.

John Carr stepped onto the conductor's podium in the bandstand and raised his baton, signaling the musicians to raise their instruments. With a downstroke of the conductor's baton, the band started playing "Donkey Serenade".

The tune was familiar, one I'd heard as a child while watching Jeanette MacDonald and Alan Jones in an old western. Brandi and Sherry started walking in different directions and had soon covered all the open area, then retraced their steps. The flutes played a light solo that I remembered hearing as a child. The crowd shouted encouragement when the alpacas crossed the square with their number, and everyone seemed to be enjoying themselves.

The band was playing "Donkey Serenade" the second time through, and the crowd was getting restless. Kerry had been standing on the opposite side of the bingo square from me, watching the crowd. His quick motion caught my eye and distracted me from the alpacas. Following his gaze, I saw two teenage boys jogging away from the bingo grid. I wondered what they were up to but assumed Kerry had the situation under control.

I looked away from Kerry when the crowd started cheering. Not knowing where the alpacas were standing, I had to look around the square. Brandi looked concerned and seemed focused across the area where Sherry's alpaca seemed to be nervously shifting his feet. Sherry was struggling to keep Doc moving ahead. The crowd, seeing Doc's tail rise, started cheering, anticipating the first winning poo deposit.

Brandi yelled something I couldn't understand, and I looked away from Sherry and Doc to see what caused Brandi's outcry. A moment later, I felt like a dozen tiny paintballs had struck me simultaneously. Startled, I looked down at dark stains on my shirt and pants. A dozen bean-sized pellets lay at my feet. The woman next to me screamed and covered her child's face as we were pelted with another barrage of alpaca poo.

Screaming spread through the crowd and I looked toward Brandi, who was trying to lead Donner in my direction. The alpaca dug her feet in and raised his tail.

I yelled, "Brandi, aim him away from the band!"

She struggled to hear me over the crowd noise. "What?"

"Turn Donner. Point his butt away from the bandshell."

Finally grasping what I was telling her, she turned Donner a second before he sprayed the crowd with pellets of alpaca poo.

Seeing only the chaos, and not the cause, Sherry yelled, "What's going on, Brandi?"

"Run to the gate! We've got to get them into the trailer!"

I pulled the crime scene tape down and cleared a path to the back of the trailer. "What's happening?" I asked as Brandi passed.

"I think they've got diarrhea!"

Screaming from the crowd continued, while the tempo of the music picked up. Sherry continued marching Doc around the square, while looking to me for direction. Seeing Doc's tail rise, I yelled, "Turn him away from the band!"

I quickly realized the error in my command when Sherry gently pulled Doc's halter so he was facing away from the band, effectively aiming his butt at the bandshell. A second later, there was another round of screams as the sound of alpaca pellets hitting brass instruments rang out.

"He got the trombones and trumpets!" someone yelled as the music died.

I jumped aside as Brandi pushed the first alpaca into the trailer. A metallic flash caught my attention. I reached down, picking up an empty Ex-Lax laxative package. I stepped around Brandi's pickup and yelled at Sherry, "Bring Doc to the trailer, Sherry. Someone fed him a laxative."

"What?" she yelled back.

"Doc's got the shits! Run to the trailer!"

To her credit, Sherry pulled Doc to the trailer. With the alpacas in the trailer and the ramp closed, a rattle of alpaca poo hit the metal ramp. Brandi bent over with her hands on her knees. "That's never happened before."

I held up the laxative package. "The alpacas have probably never eaten Ex-Lax before."

Her look of confusion changed to anger. "Who in hell would feed ex-lax to an alpaca?"

Kerry appeared with his hands on the shoulders of the two teenage boys I'd seen feeding something to the alpacas before Brandi intervened. "Will the alpacas suffer any permanent illness from eating a chocolate-flavored laxative? I've heard that chocolate is deadly for dogs."

"I don't know," Brandi replied. "I'll have to call my vet."

Sherry looked at me and started laughing.

"What?"

"You've got brown poo spots on your shirt and pants."

An older man I recognized from the Norwegian Lutheran church slapped me on the back. "Well, dam the beavers, you got splattered with alpaca *akterdekk.*"

I mouthed *akterdekk* to Brandi. She started laughing. "That's Norwegian for poop."

Meg approached me, alternately sipping water and spitting it into the grass. "I expected the alpacas to drop poop onto the squares, not shoot it horizontally."

Brandi reached up and wiped a bit of alpaca poo from the corner of Meg's mouth. "Some kids fed the alpacas Ex-Lax."

Swishing her mouth with water for the third or fourth time, Meg glared at me. "I don't suppose we know which square is the winner?"

I glanced at the grid. "I think most of the poo flew out of the contest area. I don't suppose there was an *'all-other'* category?"

Meg bit her lip. "I think you need to count the pellets in all the squares. We'll award the prize for the square with the most pellets."

Sherry giggled. "I think there are more pellets inside the Sousaphone than there are in any of the squares. The Sousaphone's big brass bell was like a giant funnel."

I leaned over so I could look into the bandshell. It was mostly empty, except for the drummers and Brian. "I think you won, Brian. The Sousaphone collected more pellets than any of the bingo squares."

Brian, who was perpetually cheerful, glared at me. "Not funny, Peter. I don't know how I'll get all the alpaca poop out of my tuba."

"There must be a joke there somewhere," I replied.

Brian cracked a smile. "Hmm. How do you clean alpaca poop out of a tuba? I'll have to work on a punchline."

Sherry gestured for me to follow her. "Come on, Peter. Let's count pellets to find out who won."

I walked parallel to Sherry, with my head down. "I think this is going to be pretty straightforward. Most of the pellets flew into the crowd."

"Here's a square next to the stage with six pellets in it," Sherry announced. "I bet these bounced off the trombone players and fell back into the square."

When we were well away from the crowd, I asked, "How is your penance going?"

"I think it's pretty much over. Everyone seems to have moved onto more pressing sins."

"More pressing sins?"

"There are all kinds of satanic symbols involved in Halloween celebrations. The ladies group is focused on them."

"What are the men focused on?" I asked.

Sherry stopped walking, causing me to look up. "You've heard about the Bigfoot sighting up by Brimson, right?"

"That's news to me."

"Well, the men's group brought in a couple of coon hounds and they're planning to comb the woods tonight."

"Please tell me that they're not planning to shoot Bigfoot."

"I think the plan is to discredit the whole sighting. They're pretty sure the sighting was Howie Almquist wearing an old beaver skin coat."

"Isn't Howie the hermit who lives in an old farmhouse?"

Sherry started walking again as we spoke. "I really don't know. I just overheard some of the teenage boys talking about it."

"You're not hanging around with the teenage boys, are you?"

"The whole nude modeling thing changed my social dynamic in the church. None of the young women my age will have anything to do with me because too many of the men are giving me too much attention. I'll be glad when my penance is through so I can go back to the dorm. Nobody cares if I model in the nude when I'm at college."

"I'm not surprised that the single men are noticing you."

Sherry stopped and stared at me like I had missed something. "Peter, it's not the *single* men who are the problem."

I kept walking, hoping to avoid making a scene. "I thought there was a commandment about not coveting."

"Yeah, it's right there alongside the one against adultery. I suppose a woman who's willing to model in the nude presents a temptation beyond the bounds of the ten commandments."

"Your father's congregation is pretty...narrow-minded."

Sherry snorted. "The Pope is narrow-minded. My father's congregation is close-minded. Anything that's spelled out as wrong in the Bible is a sin, along with anything that the Bible doesn't mention but comes to my dad's mind."

"He considers things the Bible doesn't mention sins?"

"My dad says the Bible omits things that are too heinous to be mentioned as sins."

"Things like modeling for an art class."

Sherry stopped. "I think I found the winning square. There's a whole glob of poop stuck together, like a hundred pieces. It's all in square number 74."

"And here's another smaller glob in square 62."

Sherry looked at the adjoining squares. "I can't imagine there are two other squares with more poop than this."

I kicked the two lumps of poop, causing them to break into pellets that dispersed over a large area. "Let's walk the rest of the square just to make sure."

"Why did you kick the lumps?" Sherry asked,

"Plausible deniability."

"Huh?"

"I can't imagine that any lumps we encounter will be larger than those two."

Sherry giggled. "I think kicking the lumps was a sin."

"Really? You don't think the Bible covers the proper handling of poop during alpaca bingo?"

"I may convert to your church. You seem much more open-minded than the Svenka-Gotters."

"Sherry, everyone is more open-minded than the members of the Svenska Gotter Church."

Meg was waiting for us at the bottom of the bandshell stairs looking nervous. "Do we have winners?"

"Squares 74 and 62 are the winners."

Meg nodded, then hesitated. "You're certain? There was a lot of poop flying."

I gestured toward Sherry. "We walked the whole square, and those two squares had the biggest lumps of poop."

Sherry giggled, then nodded her agreement.

Meg licked her lips. "Will those results hold up to an audit, Sherry?"

"Peter kicked all the lumps so there's no way to check."

A devious smile crept across Meg's face. "I love that plan."

After climbing the bandshell steps, Meg turned on the microphone and announced the results. There were cheers and boos, but overall, alpaca bingo was a success.

Standing near the steps going to the basement of the bandshell, Brian looked troubled. "What's wrong?" I asked.

"I must have COVID. I was pelted with alpaca poop, but I can't smell it."

Lifting my shirt, I sniffed one of the spots where I'd been hit with a pellet. "I don't smell anything, either." I turned toward the trailer, where Brandi and Sherry were having an earnest discussion. I lifted my stained shirt and sniffed it. "Brandi, we don't smell the alpaca poop."

"Alpaca manure is odorless. It's highly sought after by urban gardeners because it's natural but doesn't smell like cattle or sheep manure."

Brain laughed. "That's some consolation because every nook and cranny of the bandshell has alpaca pellets in it."

Sherry and I cleared a lane through the people lingering in the park so Brandi could drive out. "Are we done, Peter?"

"I think so. Alpaca bingo was the last activity of the day."

"Thanks."

I must've frowned. "Why are you thanking me?"

"This was a really nice break from the silent treatment I've been getting at home and at church." Sherry paused, "Meg said you were a gentleman. I had kinda known that. You didn't stare at my body while I was modeling. You proved it again today. Your wife is a lucky woman."

"There are nice guys your age, Sherry."

"I sometimes wonder."

"A dog breeder once told me to avoid buying the puppy that raced to me, leaving the rest of the litter behind. That's the alpha dog, and he'll be a problem. Pick the lonely puppy who's shivering in the corner by itself. That pup will love you like none of the others."

"Are you saying that men are like puppies?"

"I'm saying that you sometimes have to find that puppy who's too shy to race after you to find the one who's worthy of your love."

"That's pretty heavy philosophy. How did you get so smart?"

"I might've been the nerdy guy who was afraid to ask a girl on a date."

Sherry's skeptical look lingered until she finally said, "I can't believe you were ever afraid to do anything."

"Believe it. Ask my wife who suggested we go to a movie."

"She asked you out?"

"Yep. She was way too pretty and confident to ask on a date. I was embarrassed to say hi to her when we passed in the hallway."

"Huh."

"I can see the wheels turning in your brain," I said.

"There's a guy in my sociology class who's really shy. I mean, Kaden seems nice, but he's never said more than hello to me."

"Offer to buy him a cup of hot chocolate and see what happens."

"Thanks, Peter."

Sherry turned to leave, but I stopped her. "Don't let the Svenska Gotters, or anyone else, define you. If you want to pose for an art class, do it."

I was startled when Meg brushed against me. "You're not going to win any popularity contests with Sherry's parents or church."

"I'm not much of a popularity contest sort of guy."

"That's good, because I think you just gave Sherry the best parental guidance she's ever had."

"But..."

"Her parents are totally tied up in the church. Her mother is expected to be as involved as her father, which doesn't leave a lot of time for anything but yelling about things that aren't right. Sherry needs some gentle encouragement or she's going to rebel against the tight reins her parents have on her."

"Have you spoken to her, Meg?"

"I've offered her encouragement when I felt she needed it." Meg chuckled. "I may have been the one who suggested that she talk to the art studio about modeling. Not that I suggested that she strip off her clothes and model nude. She has a cute face and a nice figure. I thought she'd make a great model."

"She's the new intern."

Meg looked surprised. "Sherry is working at Whistling Pines?"

"She took a part-time position as the recreation intern."

"Do you see that becoming something permanent after she graduates?"

"I really haven't thought that far ahead. Right now, she's filling a need and she's great with the senior citizen residents."

"Are you starting art classes?" Meg asked with a sly grin.

"If we do, there won't be any nude models."

Putting her hand on my arm, Meg nodded toward a group of the Svenska Gotters in the Booya line. "I'd make that point very clear to her father, the pastor." Meg paused. "Very clear."

"I'll leave that up to Sherry."

"Pastor Vogel blames you for his daughter's modeling career. I think it would be wise if you personally explained Sherry's job responsibilities."

Watching the group of Svenska Gotters laughing, I shook my head. "I think a discussion with the pastor would go better when he wasn't with a pack of his followers."

Meg snorted. "You're not up to confronting a *pack* of Svenska Gotters?"

"I think one-on-one would be a better ratio."

Chapter 17

I was shutting down my computer when my desk phone rang. The caller ID read "THNLC", which was rather cryptic.

"Hi, Peter. I'd hoped to catch you before you left for home."

"Pastor Olafson?"

"Ron, please. Say, we're having an impromptu meeting of the um…Men's Club…if you get my drift. My office at 7:00. Bring the usual two-dollar donation to the children's library."

The *Lutheran Men's Club* was a euphemism for a group of veterans with PTSD who got together in the pastor's office to play low stakes poker. More importantly, it was a place where we could open up and speak freely with other veterans who'd experienced the horrors of battle. "Let me check with Jenny. I don't recall any other commitments for tonight."

"Great! I'll call Chief Stone to check his availability."

After ending my call with the pastor, I walked to the nursing office where Jenny was looking at a resident's medical chart on her computer. "I've been invited to the Lutheran Men's Club meeting tonight."

Jenny turned the computer screen so I couldn't see it, as required by HIPAA rules. "We've got nothing special going on. Have fun." She started to turn back toward the computer, then looked at me over her shoulder. "Is it your turn to bring the...coffee flavoring?"

The 'coffee flavoring' was a euphemism for the dollops of liquor we poured into the coffee we drank in the pastor's office. "Probably. I'll stop by the liquor store on the way to the meeting."

My cell phone rang as I walked to my car. This time the caller ID showed THPD, which was most likely Kerry calling from the police station. "Hi Kerry."

"I'm bringing the bait shop fire pictures to the men's club meeting. Maybe those guys will spot something we've missed."

"Is that legal? I mean, showing crime scene photos to a bunch of civilians?"

"That group can't be categorized as civilians. They're all soldiers who've seen worse things than the inside of a burned-out store."

"But they're not cops, Kerry."

"Which is why their eyes might spot something that a cop isn't looking for."

"It's your call. I'm stopping at the liquor store to buy a bottle of Bailey's Irish Crème for the coffee. Should I buy something as your contribution, too?"

"Sure. How about a bottle of Irish Mist. It'll complement your Irish Crème."

"You will repay me, right?"

"Of course, I will. I'll make sure I've got cash before I leave the house."

"I've had to pay the tab at Judy's the last three times because you didn't have any cash."

"And that was very kind of you. I appreciate your generosity."

"Stop buttering me up and show up with cash for the booze and your poker chips."

* * *

I slipped out of the house at 6:45 after washing the supper dishes. The liquor store was empty, and Betty, the chubby night clerk, showed me where to find the two bottles of liquor. "These are great together," she said, pointing to their locations on upper shelves of the liqueur section. "Drop an ice cube into a lowball glass, then pour an ounce of each over the ice."

"Thanks for the hint. I think we'll be serving them in coffee."

Betty led me to the counter. "That sounds yummy. It'd be even better with a whipped cream topping. It'd be a fancy Irish coffee."

"I think that touch would be wasted on the group I'm meeting."

Betty nodded as she rang up the purchase and put the bottles into paper bags. "Ah," she chuckled, "you're drinking with a group of men."

There were four vehicles in the church parking lot including the MN Department of Natural Resources pickup driven by Kevin Jenkins, the conservation officer. I carried my bag through the empty church hallways to the open door where light spilled into the dark hallway.

Ron Olafson was counting out stacks of poker chips while Kevin Jenkins, in uniform, poured coffee into mugs sitting on a tray. August (Augie) Heinz, a local farmer and former Marine, sat at the table with a small stack of dollar bills in front of him. He noted my bags, then looked over his shoulder at Kevin. "Don't overfill the mugs. Peter brought something to flavor the coffee."

I removed the bottles from the bags and set them on the pastor's conference table, which we used as a poker table for our infrequent meetings. "The Irish Mist is from Kerry. I'm providing the Bailey's Irish Crème. Betty, at the liquor store, suggested pouring equal parts of each into your coffee."

Kevin frowned. "I kind of like a dollop of whipped cream on top of my Irish Coffee."

"Yeah, Betty suggested that, but I think of a whipped cream topping as more of a girly thing."

Kevin tipped his head down, so he was looking at me over the top of his glasses. "Are you saying Marines are girly, Peter?"

Kevin watched me squirm, while I tried to frame a response to dig myself out of the hole I'd apparently created. "Um, no. I just don't think of Marines as whipped cream kind of people."

Kevin broke out laughing as he pushed his glasses up onto the bridge of his nose. "I was wondering how you were going to recover from that, sailor boy."

Kerry walked in just in time to catch Kevin needling me. He set a large manila envelope on the credenza next to the door and hung his jacket over the back of the one unoccupied chair. "What have I missed besides the Marine messing with the sailor?"

"Ante up your two bucks," the pastor said as he slid stacks of poker chips to each of us.

Kerry took out his wallet with his scarred hand and threw two dollars on the table.

He was about to put his wallet away when I cleared my throat. "Your Irish Mist cost twenty-five dollars, with tax."

Feigning surprise, Kerry pried open his wallet. "Golly, I seem to have forgotten to bring more cash. I'll pay you back the next time we go to Judy's." He hesitated, then took out thirty dollars and handed it to me. "That should cover one of the times I stuck you with Judy's bill."

Augie, a huge man who walked with a limp due to Iraq wounds, slapped the table. "Imagine that, a soldier actually settled up his bar tab with a sailor. I guess the world must be coming to an end."

Kevin, who'd served with the Army in Kosovo and Iraq, sat down, shaking his head.

"Let's play poker before the inter-service rivalry comes to blows."

Pastor Olafson, who'd been an Army chaplain, serving two tours in Iraq, shuffled a deck of cards. He dealt cards face up until Kevin received an ace. "The first ace deals. Pick your game."

Kevin gathered the cards and shuffled them. "Seven card stud. Ante a white chip."

The poker game went into its second hour. The discussion had wandered through local politics, the town's Halloween festivities, and eventually to the bait shop fire. When Kerry won a hand, earning him the dealership, he put the cards aside and reached for the envelope he'd brought. "Kevin, please refill the mugs. I've got something that requires your input, and discretion."

Augie stood and walked to the peg where he'd hung his jacket. "This sounds serious, like we should switch from Peter's foo-foo booze to something more serious." He set a bottle of Bushmills Irish Whiskey on the table and removed the cap.

Olafson shook his head. "This is a Norwegian Lutheran church. Someone should bring a bottle of aquavit."

Augie snorted as he poured generous amounts of Irish whiskey in each coffee mug. "Pastor, the last time I drank aquavit, I had the flavor of caraway in my mouth for three days. It took four Listerine washes to get my senses of smell and taste back."

Kerry spread crime scene photos on the table as the laughter died. "These were taken inside the bait shop after the fire. There were two points of ignition, identified by the heavier scorch marks and the gas cans on the floor."

Augie blew out a breath. "It looks like the inside of an Iraqi APC after it burned."

Kerry continued. "I've looked at these a hundred times and I just don't see anything that points me to a suspect or a motive."

Kevin leaned over the table, taking in the images. "Where did they find Antonich?"

Kerry separated two pictures from the rest. "These were taken in the basement. The body was found here, where the floor collapsed and covered the skeleton."

The conservation officer tapped one of the pictures. "I don't know if this ties to anything else, but there are shotgun shells spread around here. They look too small to be 12-gauge."

Kerry nodded. "A box of 16-gauge shells apparently fell into the basement and broke open when the floor collapsed. Most of them were here, near the remains."

Kevin sat down. "With the shotgun shell shortage, the big companies have stopped producing any shells that don't sell huge volumes. I go to a lot of gun shops and bait shops, and I haven't seen a single box of 16-gauge shotgun shells on the shelf in the last ten years."

Kerry shrugged. "That's interesting trivia, but I don't know how it's relevant to the arson case."

"I submitted a 16-gauge slug I recovered from a wolf carcass to the BCA for analysis. They said that type of slug hasn't been manufactured in that gauge for fifty years."

Kerry tipped his head back. "Shit. I just solved your wolf killing."

"What?" Kevin asked.

"When I searched Antonich's house, I found a double-barrel shotgun, in 16-gauge. There were half a dozen loose shells in his pocket. One of them was a paper-hulled slug."

Kevin sat up. "Do you still have it?"

"It's in our property room with the shotgun. Stop by the station tomorrow and you can take it for comparison."

I pulled the picture with the spilled shotgun shells to the middle of the table. "Does anyone think there's another 16-gauge shotgun in Two Harbors?"

Augie nodded. "I'm sure there are a few in dusty closets, but probably none that have been fired in the past twenty years. The shells are too expensive when you can find them."

Nodding, I pointed to the shells spread randomly on the floor near the skeletal remains. "I'll bet a bottle of Irish whiskey that Elmer Antonich was at the bait shop to buy the only box of 16-gauge shells in the region."

Kerry gathered up the photos. "That's possible, but I don't see how that gets us any closer to identifying the arsonist. The bait shop had been closed for hours before the fire started."

"The store was closed. But the arsonist had opened the door to light the fire. Maybe Antonich walked in thinking the store was open."

Augie shook his head. "Elmer was a civic-minded citizen, and a scrappy son of a bitch. What if he saw the door open and walked in to confront a burglar?"

"Who would walk in on a burglar?" Kerry asked. "I'd expect someone witnessing a crime to step back and call us. Maybe they would record the burglar's license number, or his description. I don't expect private citizens, especially senior citizens, to confront a burglar."

Augie chuckled. "I knew Elmer pretty well. He had a reputation for resolving hockey disputes with his fists. He probably thought of himself as that same scrappy SOB he'd been in the '60s. Hell, he could probably beat any of us in a bare knuckles fight. I don't think he'd hesitate to walk into a burglary and expect to beat the snot out of the punk burglar."

"I don't see how that gets me any closer to solving the arson," Kerry replied.

"Did anyone see a burglar walking around town with a black eye in the days after the fire?" Augie asked. "Was there blood on Elmer's knuckles when his body was found?"

Kerry silently slid the pictures back into the envelope. "I'll call the ME and BCA tomorrow. We weren't specifically looking for blood when we examined the body or crime scene."

Chapter 18

Kerry walked into my office shortly after nine o'clock the next morning. "Buy me a cup of coffee."

I looked at the piles of paper scattered on my desktop. "I was trying to..."

Kerry nodded toward the door. "Let's walk down to the dining room."

I stacked the pile I was working on and set it next to the computer, then followed him down the hallway. "You never want to have coffee in our dining room. What changed?"

"Someone here knows an arsonist."

I stopped walking. "What?"

"Your residents have lived in town all their lives and most of them know every person in town. I'd say that the odds are that several of them know the arsonist, and one of them probably even knows that he's lighting the fires."

"I doubt that. None of them have been in town other than to eat pie at Judy's Café in the past couple of years."

"The arsonist isn't a teenager, Peter. It's someone who's lit several fires. Arsonists don't retire after their first fire. They get hooked on the excitement."

The dining room was nearly empty between breakfast and lunch. Four women were playing bridge near the windows, Wendy was tapping her pencil on a rear table while contemplating a crossword puzzle answer, and two men were having a quiet discussion at a table near the coffee urn. I drew two mugs of coffee from the urn as Kerry approached the two men.

Howard Johnson nodded to Kerry as I approached, then introduced his companion. "Chief Stone, this is Ben 'Butter' Jacobson."

Kerry shook hands with both men. "Why do they call you Butter?" Kerry asked as he sat.

Butter, who was a few pounds past obese smiled. "I was the half-back on the football team. I could slip through the opposing players like butter."

Howard, the voice of sanity in a place where truth and diplomacy were often in short supply, laughed. "That was fifty years ago, Butter. I think that nickname stuck because you sold used cars and your salesmanship was legendary, the list of a car's features slipped out of your mouth as smooth as butter."

"Are you accusing me of lying?"

Howard leaned close to Kerry, who accepted a steaming mug of coffee from me. "Let's say Butter always offered a thread of truth with his sales pitches."

"I resent that!"

Leaning back, Howard smiled. "Butter, you were a used car salesman. People expected you to stretch the truth."

Butter picked up the spoon he'd used to stir cream into his coffee and fingered it. "I made a living selling cars. I always paid my mortgage, fed my family, and kept the kids in new shoes. I sold cars to generations of families, and rarely had a complaint."

I interrupted the discussion. "Kerry has a serious police problem. He asked me to introduce him to some of the people of sound mind, who've lived in Two Harbors their entire lives. You two fit those requirements."

Howard grasped his coffee mug in both hands. "Fire away, Chief."

"Actually, fire is the topic I'd like to discuss. I'm sure you've heard about the bait shop fire. It's no secret that the local fire marshal determined that it was arson."

Butter held his cup out to me. "Could you get me a refill, Peter? I'd like a dollop of cream in it."

I took both Butter and Howard's mugs to the urn and filled them with coffee, as Kerry explained how the arson determination had been made. Returning to the table, I set the mugs in front of Howard and Butter as Kerry wrapped up.

"What do you want from us?" Butter asked as he stirred his coffee.

"I understand that this isn't the first business to burn down under suspicious circumstances."

Howard sipped his coffee, then drew a breath. "There have been a number of business fires over the years. I don't know if any of them were considered arson."

Butter, who was usually outspoken, focused on his coffee without saying anything.

"I went back through the police department files and found seven fires over the past forty years that were suspicious. Two more were definitely arson. No one has ever been arrested in any of those cases."

Twitching his nose as if he was about to sneeze, Butter looked troubled. He glanced at his watch. "Heck, it's almost time for my show."

Kerry put his hand on Butter's arm as he pushed his chair back to stand. "It's a quarter to ten. No television shows will start for at least fifteen minutes."

"Yeah, I've got to get comfortable and adjust the blinds, so the sun isn't shining on the television."

"How many of those nine fires do you know about, Butter?" Kerry asked.

"There are fires in town all the time." He nodded. "All the time."

"Most of the business fires seemed to occur in places that were having financial issues."

"Coincidence," Butter replied.

"At least two of them were restaurant grease fires," Howard said,

Nodding, Kerry smiled. "Grease fires that started hours after the deep fryers and grills were shut down. There shouldn't have been any heat to start a fire in the wee hours of the morning."

"Spontaneous combustion," Butter said. "Some fires just ignite."

"Not without a spark," Kerry countered.

"That lumberyard fire probably started in a smoldering pile of sawdust," Butter replied.

Kerry let go of Butter's arm and leaned back. "It's funny that you should mention the lumberyard fire. That was more than fifty years ago and the file from the investigation was very thin. There was a note about the fire starting near a saw, but no one determined the exact location of the fire or the ignition source."

Howard leaned back and stared at the ceiling, deep in thought. "That was one heck of an inferno. All that dry lumber burned, and the flames were twice as high as the hotel roof. I remember thinking that every fire truck between Duluth and Lutsen was squirting water on that building. Not that they could do much except keep the fire from spreading to the entire town."

Butter continued to stare at his cup as he pushed it in circles in front of himself. "It was a darned shame."

"You were just a high school kid back then," Howard replied.

"Yeah. That was my senior year."

Butter looked like he had more to say, but he just stared at his mug.

Kerry studied Butter's demeanor. "Butter, what else do you know about the lumberyard fire?"

Looking startled by Kerry mentioning his name, Butter looked up. "That was a long time ago. The statute of limitations is long past, right?"

"It sounds like you know someone who might've been involved in the fire," Kerry said.

"Naw. I was just asking."

"If the statute of limitations has passed, and I can't arrest anyone for lighting the fire, who do you think lit it?"

"He's dead now."

Howard looked at me, then at Butter as he leaned forward. "Who's dead, Butter?"

"Jack Strandquist died on a fishing boat in the '80s."

Kerry leaned close to Butter. "Jack Strandquist started the lumberyard fire?"

Butter shrugged. "He claimed that he did. I don't know otherwise."

"Was he involved in any of the other fires?"

"His cousin, Dippy, was having problems meeting the mortgage on his restaurant. Jack claimed that he helped Dippy out."

Kerry took a pen and notebook out of his pocket. "Dippy's café burned down in 1971."

"That sounds about right," Butter replied.

"What do you know about the other fires?"

Butter slid his coffee mug to the center of the table. "Chief, I'm not saying anything more. There are hard-working business owners who just couldn't make it. Someone did them a favor by letting them collect the insurance money so they could get out of debt."

Butter pushed his chair away from the table and stood. He drew a breath, then looked between the three of us. "It serves no purpose to dig through those ashes." Then he walked away.

Expecting Kerry to go after him, I was surprised when he sat back and took another sip of coffee. "I'm confused. Why aren't you pressing Butter on the arson?"

"I think he's already told us all he's going to say."

"But he knows who set all those fires."

Howard Johnson looked at Kerry, then me. "There's more than one arsonist involved in this."

"Of course, there is," I said. "Jack Strandquist died."

Kerry stood. "Let's call it a day."

"I thought you were hot on the trail of the arsonist?" I asked. "You're just going home?"

Howard shook his head. "Take it easy, Peter. The arsonist isn't going anywhere."

"What am I missing?" I asked. "What if the arsonist decides to light another business on fire tonight?"

Kerry took my elbow and guided me to the dining room door. "There won't be any fires tonight."

"How can you be sure of that?"

"Sparky is at a fire chief's conference in Minneapolis."

I pulled Kerry aside, next to the aviary. "Sparky is the arsonist?"

"He's not the arsonist, but he's part of the show that the arsonist wants to put on for us."

"What are you talking about?"

"The arsonist likes to watch the chaos he creates. If Sparky isn't around, the assistant chief might not call for mutual aid as quickly and there won't be as much excitement."

"Do you know who the arsonist is?" I whispered.

"I have a pretty good idea of who it might be."

"Does it have something to do with Elmer Antonich dying in the bait shop?"

"In a twisted sort of way, maybe."

"Are you going to tell me?"

Kerry's eyes sparkled. "I'll make a deal with you. I'll bring you along for the arrest. Okay?"

"But not tonight?"

Kerry shook his head. "I'm going home. I encourage you to do the same. Tomorrow might be a little crazy."

* * *

I stormed into Jenny's office and closed the door. "You won't believe what Kerry did to me."

Obviously, not buying into my anger, she smiled. "What happened?"

"Kerry knows who the arsonist is. He won't tell me who he suspects, and he's just going home for supper and will deal with it tomorrow."

Jenny bit her bottom lip to suppress her laughter. "And you're upset because you're not going to sleep tonight wondering who it is."

"Well, yes. It was a cruel thing to do."

"It sounds like we should have pizza for supper."

"What does pizza have to do with anything?"

"You're too wound up to cook, and I'm behind on charts. I think you should order a pizza after you pick up Amy from daycare."

"Fine. Just for the record, I'm having a beer."

"Ooh, now there's a threat! That should teach Kerry a lesson."

I tried to give Jenny my best stink eye, but she broke out laughing. "Stop that! I'm being serious."

"No, you're being childish. Get out of here so I can finish up my charts and make a call to Dr. Bergstrom. I'll see you in an hour or so."

I stopped with the door half open. "I may order anchovies on the pizza."

"Don't even think about it. If there are anchovies on the pizza, you will sleep in your car. Besides, you don't like anchovies. You'd only do that to wind me up."

"It'd only be fair to have you as wound up as I am."

Jenny pointed at the door. "Get out of here. I'll see you in a while."

As I closed the door she added, "No anchovies."

Chapter 19

I was half awake and had barely booted up my computer when Kerry walked into my office with a trim, middle-aged man I'd seen around town. "Peter, I'd like you to meet Bruce Sanders. He owns The Body Shop in town."

I shook his hand, trying to remember where I'd seen an automotive body repair shop in town. Flashing back to my discussion with Darrel, I remembered that his son owned the only commercial exercise facility in Two Harbors.

Sensing my confusion, Bruce explained, "I've got a gym in what used to be the Ben Franklin store. You've probably seen people on the treadmills that face the front windows."

"Oh, that kind of body shop. Not the automotive body shop."

Kerry gestured for Bruce to sit in one of the two guest chairs in my cramped office. After closing the door, he sat in the other chair and leaned forward. "Bruce has been working undercover with me on the arson investigation."

"You hadn't mentioned..."

Kerry smiled. "The fewer people who know about an undercover operation, the better."

"Okay," I sat leaning back. "Why are you telling me now?"

"We're setting up a sting that's going to require around-the-clock surveillance of Bruce's shop."

Feeling confused, I asked, "So, why tell me now?"

"Because you're part of the surveillance team."

"I'm not a cop. I'm not part of whatever surveillance team you're setting up."

Waving off my protest, Kerry said, "I'm giving you first choice. Would you rather be teamed up with Sparky or Kevin Jenkins, the conservation officer?'

"I'd rather be home in bed alongside my wife."

"Sparky it is, then."

"I just refused."

"Huh," Kerry said. "I thought I heard you say you were leaving the choice of your partner up to me. I'll take the second shift with Kevin."

"You're sticking me in a car with Sparky? When?"

"We're going to start tonight after Bruce locks up."

"I close at 5:00, but I do the books and clean the equipment until 6:00."

"Realistically, the arsonist probably isn't going to strike until after dark. You and Sparky don't need to be in position until 8:00. Kevin and I will relieve you at 3:00."

I must've grimaced. "What are we supposed to do if we see the arsonist?"

"Dial 911 to request backup, then keep him under surveillance until the sheriff's department or I show up."

"I don't see this going well. Suppose he's dumping gas all over the inside of the place and ready to drop a match before you arrive."

"You're a reserve officer. Arrest him."

"Come on. I haven't been trained and I don't even own a pair of handcuffs."

Bruce was smiling, enjoying the exchange. "Yeah, Chief, he doesn't even have handcuffs."

"Trust me," Kerry replied. "He'll run as soon as you confront him."

"I'm skeptical about any comment preceded by 'trust me.'"

"The guy will run. Follow him and your backup will arrive to arrest him."

"Wow, this just gets better and better. Now, you expect me to chase this guy through downtown until someone with a badge shows up. Do you have any idea how long it's been since I was in basic training and was in condition?"

Bruce couldn't suppress his laughter any longer. "I've got this mental image of Peter and Sparky trying to keep up with some high school track star as he sprints through the alleys."

Kerry turned. "What makes you think it's some high school kid, Bruce?"

"Isn't that what you think? I mean, who besides a kid would be stupid enough to torch a building? It has to be a high school vandal. Right?"

"Did the guy who called you on the blocked phone sound like a teenager?"

"I couldn't tell. He had something over the phone, so his voice was distorted. I couldn't even tell if it was a man or a woman making the call."

"Hang on," I said. "What call are you talking about?"

Kerry waited until Bruce stopped laughing before answering. "Bruce has been in all the cafés and bars here and all the way to Silver Bay complaining about how poor his business is and how close he is to going broke."

Bruce nodded. "I've been practically crying in my beer saying I wish I could find a way out of my financial hole. Then, I get this muffled call and a guy asks if I'd be willing to pay him a thousand dollars to make my problem go away. I pretend to be mad and accuse him of being a spam call, then he suggests that he's experienced at making buildings burn down so the owner can collect the insurance. I assure him that my insurance premiums have been paid and that I owe less on the building than the insurance coverage. So, he tells me to make sure I'm out of town the next two nights, so I've got an alibi."

"He trusts that you'll pay him after the fire?"

Bruce shook his head. "I had to leave five hundred dollars in used bills under a garbage can in the park yesterday. He called back to confirm that he got the payment and assured me that my problem would be solved in one of the next two nights."

I looked at Kerry. "Why didn't you arrest him when he picked up the money?"

"He hasn't done anything illegal yet. For all I know, he could be shaking Bruce down to get the initial payment."

"You just let him pick up the money and walk away?" I asked.

"All the serial numbers on the bills have been recorded, and we have pictures of a person taking the money bag."

I nodded. "So, you followed him, and you know who it is?"

Bruce looked at Kerry, who was suddenly sheepish. "Um, we followed him until he got in a boat and motored away."

I felt my blood pressure climbing. "What's going to stop him from using the same escape strategy after he lights the fire? I'm not hurling myself into a moving boat to catch an arsonist."

Bruce's eyes sparkled. "I'd like to see a video of that!"

"The Coast Guard Reserve will have their boat idling about a hundred yards up the shore. They'll be able to intercept him if he tries to escape east on the lake."

"And if he goes west?"

"Sparky will have two guys in the fire department rescue boat near the harbor."

"What if he jumps in a car or pickup and drives away?"

"Peter, we've got it covered. Trust me."

"There's that phrase again, 'trust me.'"

"This is what I did in the Army. This is not a one-time thing for me. I know how to plan an operation like this."

"How often did the bad guys get away?"

"I wish I could say never. Not often."

"Sparky and I can only see one side of the building. What if the guy breaks in the back?"

Bruce chuckled. "He's not going to break in. Part of the deal is that I'll leave the side door unlocked. He'll bust a window as he leaves so it looks like a break in, but he'll enter through the east door."

"Kerry, every damned battle plan falls to pieces as soon as the first shot is fired. You know that as well as me."

"This is not a battle plan, and no shots will be fired. It's all planned, and it'll be simple and easy. All you have to do is dial 911, confront the guy, then follow when he runs. Hell, you can let Sparky run after him if you want to hang back. Sparky works out so he can carry the biggest fireman out of a burning structure."

"You know I can't let Sparky face whatever happens alone."

Bruce looked at Kerry. "You said Peter would have to save his buddy."

Kerry nodded. "A corpsman doesn't leave his men behind."

I threw up my arms. "When and where do I meet Sparky?"

"Pick him up at the fire station at 6:45."

"We're using *my car*?"

Kerry and Bruce stood. "Can you think of anything that looks less like a cop can than your rusty Corolla?"

"Do you have any other words of wisdom?" I asked as Kerry stepped through the door.

"Don't drink too much coffee. It's a long walk to the all-night gas station to use the restroom."

I walked to the nursing office where Jenny was speaking to one of the aides. She turned to me when the aide left. "I heard you're on arson patrol tonight."

"That's not common knowledge here is it?"

"Deb Stone called and warned me that Kerry was going to draft you for arson surveillance tonight. She offered to bring over popcorn and a movie if I wanted someone to talk to."

"Is she coming over?"

Jenny chuckled. "Who am I to refuse Deb a chance to snuggle with your cute daughter? Besides, she's good company and the boys will keep themselves occupied."

"I'm going to be trapped in the Corolla for five or six hours with Sparky. Do you have any meds for anxiety?"

Jenny snorted. "You'll be fine. Sparky is a nice guy."

"We have nothing in common."

"That's not true. He's been dating Wendy."

"Wendy did a lap dance as she sang. Sparky enjoyed it way too much."

"Anyway, they've been dating. He'll probably have some insights about Wendy that you didn't know. Maybe more discussions about the definition of second base," she chuckled.

"Trust me, I already know more about Wendy than I ever wanted to know."

Chapter 20

As promised, Deb Stone showed up with her son, a bag of popcorn, a giant tub of cheese curls, and two DVD cases with covers featuring shirtless, hunky guys—definitely not movies I would've chosen. She pecked me on the cheek as she walked past. She held up one of the movies whose cover featured a sweaty cowboy and smiled. "Are you certain you don't want to hang around to watch *Love's Furies* with us?"

"I'd rather have surgery on an ingrown toenail."

Deb leaned close and whispered, "You'll owe me big if this movie leaves your wife hungry with unfulfilled passion."

"What about you? Is Kerry going to be dealing with unfulfilled passion?"

Deb snorted and rolled her eyes. "Our days of unfulfilled passion are limited to his days off, a babysitter, and a bottle of wine."

"It's difficult to be spontaneous when you've got kids."

"It's difficult to be passionate when your husband comes home smelling of dead bodies and arson fires. Let me tell you a secret. The smell of a decaying body gets into your skin and no amount of scrubbing takes it away."

"Ouch. That'd be a romance killer."

Deb put her hand on my arm. "I never said this, but two years of skin grafts and physical therapy aren't conducive to romantic interludes either. Thanks for suggesting this job to Kerry. He's a different person now, with a purpose in his life."

"I thought the stink of dead bodies…"

Deb squeezed my arm. "That wears off. It takes longer to deal with the internal scars of battle…as you know."

Jenny swept down the staircase with Amy on her hip as the sound of a video game drifted downstairs. "What does Peter know?"

Deb held up the cheese curl tub. "How addictive these things are."

I held out my hand. "I could take them along on our surveillance and save you from the temptation."

Jenny snatched the tub away. "In your dreams, sailor. I'm planning to have near-permanent orange stains on my fingers."

Amy recognized the cheese curls and put her hand on the clear container. "It looks like all the girls like cheese curls."

Deb held the DVD case out to Jenny. "I think we should start with this one."

Jenny glanced at the cover, then flipped the case over to read the blurb on the back. "OMG, you brought this filthy smutty movie for us to watch?"

Deb's eyes lit up. "Yup."

"But the boys are upstairs…"

Deb grabbed the television remote control off the end table. "I'm the master of the quick channel switch. I'll have my finger on the button and as soon as I hear footsteps on the stairs, we'll be watching the home shopping channel."

Jenny opened the DVD case and popped the movie into the player. "You are a bad influence, Deb Stone."

"I never get to watch these at home. Kerry says they're disgusting."

Settling onto the couch, Jenny looked at me expectantly. "Are you still here?"

"If that movie is about to play, I'm out of here."

A second later the opening scene appeared on screen as a hunky cowboy rode his horse into the corral.

* * *

After topping off my gas tank, I went into the station and bought two cans of highly caffeinated soda pop, two plastic-wrapped ham and cheese sandwiches, and a jumbo bag of potato chips. While waiting for my debit card to be approved, the young clerk put everything into a plastic bag. "It looks like you're the winner of the unhealthy supper of the year award."

"I'm not eating all this myself."

The girl smiled. "I'm not judging. I had a twin-pack of Twinkies and an orange soda for supper."

"Really," I protested. About to explain I was going on a police stakeout with the fire chief, I realized how inappropriate the discussion of a confidential police operation would be with the teenage gas station clerk. Composing myself, I nodded. "I'll eat a carrot later."

With a knowing nod, the girl pushed the plastic bag across the counter to me. "Sure. That's what I tell my mom, too. She doesn't believe me, either."

Setting my purchases on the floor of the back seat, I climbed in and started the car. *It's sad when you feel the need to justify yourself to a gas station clerk.*

Sparky was sitting in the fire chief's red pickup parked outside the fire station. He saw me but didn't get out. Rolling down the window as I approached, he looked annoyed. "Climb in," he said.

"We should take my car because it looks less like a surveillance vehicle. A red pickup with a light bar on top will stand out."

"I need the pickup in case there's a fire."

I looked at the red pickup with the bar of lights across the top. "Don't you think this will stand out when we're watching for an arsonist?"

After considering my comment for a second, Sparky sighed. "I suppose there's some merit to your argument." He got out, then reached in for an old-fashioned metal lunch box and a battered thermos.

"What have you got?" I asked as he locked the pickup.

"I didn't have time for supper, so I brought something to eat, and a thermos of coffee to keep us awake until our backup arrives."

"I bought snacks, too. You can set your lunch bucket on the floor of the back seat."

The aroma of cooked cabbage was filling my car when I got in. "What's in your lunchbox?" I asked as I pulled away from the curb.

"My mom warmed up some cabbage rolls. They're swimming in tomato sauce."

Alarm bells were ringing in my head as I struggled to maintain my composure. "Um, Sparky, cabbage rolls seem like a poor choice when the two of us are cooped up inside a small car."

"There are enough for both of us."

"How does that solve the problem?" I asked.

"Well, you won't have to suffer from my gas production. You'll be creating your own stink."

A childhood adage, which had been attributed to Confucius, popped into my head. "Man who passes gas in church sits in his own pew."

Sparky threw his head back and laughed. "That's a good one, Doc."

"I prefer being called Peter."

Looking wounded, Sparky sighed. "I thought we were closer than that. I mean, I let you call me Sparky. I felt that calling you Doc was an okay thing."

"Everyone calls you Sparky."

"That's true, but not everyone uses it as a sincere sign of respect."

Trying hard to suppress laughter, I nodded while trying to respond. I'd always thought of Sparky as a derogatory nickname for an incompetent electrician or fireman.

Misinterpreting my silence for agreement, he added, "There are some town folks who use Sparky in a mean way. I'm a good person, and a good fireman. Heck, the rest of the firemen voted me in as the chief, right?"

Having been informed by Kerry that none of the other firemen wanted the headaches associated with the chief's position, I could do nothing but nod. There was nothing to be said.

"I'm a good fire chief. I respond first to the fire calls, I show the guys where to squirt the water, I make sure the fire engines get regular oil changes, I bought carnauba wax for the trucks because it holds up better. I bring coffee and doughnuts to the training sessions. I mean, what else is there for a good chief to do?"

"I can't think of an additional thing a good fire chief should do."

I circled the block facing The Body Shop, trying to find a place to park where two guys sitting in a car wouldn't scream, *these two guys are conducting surveillance*. It quickly became apparent that downtown Two Harbors wasn't a hotbed of activity at six o'clock on a weeknight. There was no one walking on the sidewalks, and I drove the only car that was moving on the streets.

"It will be difficult to be incognito," I said as I stopped on a cross street where I could see the front of The Body Shop building.

"Ah. If you cut through the parking lot, there's an alley next to the Harbor Theater. If you park there, we can see The Body Shop's front door."

I looped around the block and came into the alley from the rear. Easing ahead so the hood of my car was barely visible past the building, we could watch the entrance, and see a portion of the building's side, including an emergency exit. "I think this is the best we can do," I said.

"Yup. It helps that you haven't washed or waxed your car recently. There's no reflection from the streetlights. That was smart on your part."

Not wanting to admit that I never washed or waxed my car, I nodded. "Yeah, good planning."

Reaching behind the seat, Sparky picked up the Thermos and unscrewed the cup. "I didn't remember to bring a second cup. We'll have to share."

"That's okay. I bought myself a couple cans of soda pop."

After pouring coffee into the cup, Sparky leaned back. "It's going to be a long night. Do you know any good jokes?"

"My joke repertoire is limited to the tuba jokes supplied by Brian Johnson."

"They're all pretty sick."

"Yes, but they're clean, so I can tell my son most of them."

Gripping the thermos cup between his knees, Sparky reached into the backseat again. He opened the scarred metal lunchbox and released the latches. Removing a Tupperware container and lifting the lid it infused the car with the aroma of warm cooked cabbage. "Would you like a cabbage roll now?" He asked as he tucked a paper napkin into the neck of his shirt.

"Thanks, I think I'll wait."

Taking out a fork, Sparky separated a piece of cabbage roll and lifted it to his mouth, exposing the ground beef and rice filling. The tomato sauce dripped from the fork and onto the napkin covering his shirt.

"Mmm. You don't know what you're missing."

I focused on the buildings down the street, trying to ignore the slurping and yummy sounds Sparky made as he ate.

Snapping shut the plastic container, Sparky said, "You did a nice job at Hugo's the other night. I really enjoyed the band."

I thought back to the performance and Sparky's group of rowdy firemen seated at a table in the front row. Then, I recalled Wendy's flirtatious version of "Unchained Melody" sung while sitting on Sparky's lap. "I could see how Wendy's performance enhanced your enjoyment."

"Your friend Wendy is really something. And her tattoos. Whew, some of them are pretty...revealing. She showed me the one on her..."

I grimaced. "Please. I have to work with Wendy and I really don't want to know any more about her tattoos than I have already seen."

"But the Leprechaun..."

"Stop, Sparky. Do not describe the Leprechaun."

"It's not so much the Leprechaun as the rainbow and pot of gold."

"No, Sparky. I don't want to know about the Leprechaun or the pot of gold."

"You have to follow the rainbow..."

"No, Sparky. No Leprechaun, pot of gold, or rainbow. Move on to another topic."

Reveling in my discomfort, Sparky got a mischievous grin. "I've got a tattoo."

I grimaced. "I'd prefer to talk about other topics. I don't need to know about your tattoo either."

Chapter 21

We were startled by a knock on Sparky's window. Wendy grinned at me for one second before she opened the rear door and climbed into the backseat. "Hi guys. I heard you were looking for a party."

I glared at Sparky. "This is supposed to be a secret undercover operation. You told Wendy about it?"

"She's the only person I told."

"We weren't supposed to tell anyone."

Wendy leaned forward so her face was between us. "I'll bet you told Jenny."

"Of course, I told Jenny. She's watching the kids while I'm hanging out with Sparky."

"See," Wendy replied. "Why shouldn't Sparky tell me? We're an item."

"What?" I asked. I turned to glare at Wendy but realized that move put our noses about an inch apart. I quickly turned back. "Since when are you two an item?"

"Since the band's gig at Hugo's. Sparky hung around after we packed up and we..."

"That's really more than I needed to know." Scrunching my nose in disgust, I tried to expel any recollection of the lasagna dinner conversation Jenny and I had experienced with Sparky regarding the "bases," and which two he had visited with Wendy in Hugo's parking lot.

"Come on, Peter," Wendy chided. "We're consenting adults."

"That's still too much information."

Changing the topic, Wendy said, "Sparky, I got a new tattoo." I heard the sound of a zipper in the back seat.

Sparky twisted in his seat to view the tattoo Wendy was revealing. I tried to remain uninvolved, but couldn't help looking in the mirror, getting a glimpse of cupid pulling his bow as Wendy lifted her shirt and lowered the waistband of her jeans.

Sparky was engrossed. "You're not wearing underwear?"

Shifting so a strip of lacy red appeared, Wendy said, "I'm wearing a thong. I thought it might fit better with our plans for later."

I shouldn't have been surprised by Wendy's lack of modesty. "All right," I said. "I'm right here."

Wendy looked at me in the mirror and smiled. "I know."

"But you keep going."

"Just look away, Peter."

"It's my car and whatever happens in the back seat is my business. Please pull up your jeans."

Sparky saw me staring into the mirror and chuckled. "So, you're a voyeur."

"I am NOT a voyeur. Wendy, stop doing whatever you're doing. Sparky, focus on The

Body Shop and resume your undercover duties."

Wendy giggled. "Undercover duties. I like the sound of that."

I twisted in the seat, so I was staring at Wendy. "Stop distracting him before I call Kerry and report you for indecent exposure!"

"Take it easy," Wendy replied as she pulled up and zipped her jeans.

"Sparky, focus. If the arsonist appears, we need to be ready to jump into action."

"If something happens, I'll catch up with you," Sparky protested.

"I don't want you to 'catch up to me' while I am wrestling with an arsonist. I want you beside me."

Sparky turned back toward the windshield. "To tell you the truth, I was never really clear on what would happen if we actually saw the arsonist. I'm not interested in getting burned, shot, stabbed, punched, or even bruised. I thought we'd take pictures and hand them over to the chief."

"We're trying to stop an arson fire. Prevention might mean intervening while the crime is in progress."

Wendy perked up. "Let me chase him down. Bad guys don't punch women."

"Where the hell did you hear that lie?" I asked.

"Peter, haven't you ever watched a television police show? The guy cop always gets beat up and the female cop calls it in and maybe maces the criminal. She rarely gets her uniform dirty.”

“That’s fiction! We’re dealing with a real live criminal who intends to burn the place down. People like that don’t want to go to prison. They resist arrest, fight, punch, and run away.”

“I kind of like the photograph idea,” Sparky repeated. “We get a picture of the guy and let the police actually make the arrest.”

“Did you bring a camera, Sparky?” I asked.

“There’s a camera built into my cell phone.”

I was about to point out the shortcomings of using a cell phone camera to take pictures of an arsonist across the street, without a telephoto lens, in low light, when Wendy whispered, “Look! There’s someone in the alley.”

The Navy and Marines told me repeatedly that there are two kinds of situations: One situation is best dealt with by taking a second to assess your surroundings before acting. In that case, you could avoid walking into an ambush or tripping an explosion. The other situation called for you to act without thinking. That occurred when you were under fire. You jumped behind whatever cover you could find. From there, you assessed your situation and decided whether to stay put, move, or exercise your third option. That third option was kissing your ass goodbye as all hell exploded around you.

I was reaching for the door handle when Sparky hissed, "Wait. Turn off the dome light so it doesn't give us away."

"Great suggestion, Sparky. Why didn't you suggest that when we were sitting here waiting for something to happen?"

"It just occurred to me."

"How do I turn off the dome light?" I asked, looking at the assorted knobs and switches in front of me in the dim light provided by the streetlights.

"It's in your operator's manual," Wendy suggested.

Feeling like I was cast in *Dumb and Dumber 3*, I looked at Wendy in the mirror. "I can't reach the glove compartment. If one of us gets out of the car, the dome light will come on when the door opens."

Wendy reached up and touched the overhead light. "My car has a setting where I can shut off the overhead light by pushing a button alongside the light." Before I could stop her, Wendy reached for the overhead light and pushed a button. The light came on. "Oops. Wrong button."

"Come on," I said, pushing my door open and stepping into the alley.

Blinded by the bright light in the car, it took my eyes a second to adjust to the dark alley. I moved ahead with my hand against a brick wall, while trying to see the dark figure who'd been in the alley across the street. I heard Sparky's door open as he and Wendy scrambled out of the car.

"Why aren't you running after him?" Wendy asked.

"Because I was blinded by the light you turned on, Wendy."

"He was across the street," she whispered.

"I know that. I can't see across the street."

"Oof," I heard from the opposite side of the car. "Damned potholes!" Sparky swore as he tripped in the dark alley.

Abandoning any attempt at stealth, I jogged the few steps to the nearest sidewalk, then hesitated, looking into the opposite alley as my eyes adjusted to the dim light provided by the streetlamps. Unable to discern anything or anyone across the street, I trotted across the sidewalk and street, then across the opposite sidewalk before reaching the alley. I stopped at the store front and peeked around the corner as Wendy and Sparky ran across the street, with Sparky swearing under his breath about the pothole that had tripped him in the alley.

Motioning with my hand in an attempt to get Sparky to shut up, I caught Wendy's attention. Not knowing the Marine Corps' gesture for quiet, Wendy mistook my hand signal for a stop sign, and she froze abruptly, halfway across the street, causing Sparky to run into her. That generated another string of profanity as they staggered and fell in the middle of the street, lit by a streetlamp on the corner, one half a block away.

Alternately hoping that the arsonist had run away, then hoping he wasn't standing in the alley with a gun pointed at me, I stepped into the alley, then ducked to my right, hoping to distract a potential shooter from Wendy and Sparky, who were now arguing as they untangled themselves in the street.

The alley appeared empty aside from a dumpster, but I heard the sound of running footsteps somewhere ahead of me. "Sparky, run to the end of the block and cut off the guy who's running away," I shouted as I sprinted down the alley after the arsonist.

"Which way? Left, or right?" Sparky replied.

"One of you go in each direction," I yelled over my shoulder.

"Good plan," Sparky replied as he sprinted to the right.

The alley ended at the next street. I stopped, looking both directions for the arsonist. Seeing no one, I listened for the sound of footsteps, but heard nothing. I dialed 911, identified myself, and explained that Chief Stone was expecting my call.

A moment later, Kerry's distorted voice was patched from his radio to my phone. "What's up?"

"We spooked the arsonist, and he ran. I chased him down an alley behind The Body Shop, but there's no sign of him in either direction."

"Is Sparky with you?"

"He and Wendy were with me. We split up and ran in three different directions. Sparky went to the right and Wendy went left. They should show up at the opposite ends of the block shortly."

"Why is Wendy with you?"

"It's a long story."

"Where are you?"

"I'm a block south of where we'd been parked."

There was a pause as Kerry groaned. "Which street are you on?"

"I can't see a street sign. I'm a block over from The Body Shop."

Kerry sighed. "Give me the name of a store near you."

"I'm between Stonebrook's law office and the butcher shop."

"Stay there. I'm on my way."

With the call ended, I held the phone in my hand, while pondering the disappearance of the arsonist. My thoughts were disrupted by a woman's scream to my left. Sprinting in the direction of the scream, Kerry's admonition to wait where I was seemed irrelevant.

There was another scream, then shouting as I neared the corner. Without checking first, I ran around the corner and was hit like a football player who was blindsided by another player tackling him. Flying through the air, I landed on my butt, with my head snapping back and striking the sidewalk. I felt the weight of a body on top of me. That person scrambled to get up.

"Damn you!" Wendy screamed a second before I felt a doubling of the weight on top of me. "Hold still or I'll..."

Her words were lost in the grunts and gasps emitted on top of me, not that I noticed. The runner's shoulder had impacted my solar plexus during the initial impact. While knocking the air from my lungs, it had also rendered me unable to inhale. Seconds after that, I rolled onto my stomach and I tried to crawl away. The combination left my brain screaming for oxygen, while unable to process what was happening in the struggle taking place on top of me as my body, then face were ground into the sidewalk.

While struggling to free myself, I saw a flash in the alley I'd just left. A moment later, I felt, as much as heard, WHOOSH as the pressure from a mini explosion in the alley reached the street.

I had no time to contemplate the situation. Being ground into the sidewalk, I tried to push the people off me, thinking that their wrestling was somehow responsible for my inability to breathe. Pushing and thrashing my legs failed to move the pile. Stars flashed in my eyes as my brain screamed for a breath. With one great push-up, I managed to relieve the pressure long enough to take a shallow breath. A moment later, I heard Sparky yelling Wendy's name. Hoping that he'd pull the bodies off the pile on top of me, I stopped struggling. Instead of relief, I felt more weight as Sparky apparently jumped onto the pile. I could no longer budge the wriggling, elbowing, swearing pile. Someone jammed a knee into my ribs, causing a sharp pain that forced me to release the breath I was holding. My view went from the dimly lit street, to sparkling points of light, to darkness, as consciousness slipped away.

My next memory was Kerry yelling at someone. "I've got an ambulance coming."

Sparky's response didn't register, but I felt someone place their fingers on my neck, apparently checking for my pulse.

"Sweet baby Jesus," I whispered. "I'm alive. Leave me alone."

Wendy's nervous laugh irritated me. "Good job, Sparky. You got a rise out of him."

Taking inventory of my situation, I tried to reason through what was going on. My memory was limited to the pressure of the scramble on top of me after someone, maybe the arson suspect, knocked me down. "Help me get up." I said, trying to push myself upright with my elbows.

Gentle pressure on my shoulder kept me down as Kerry said, "Stay put until the EMTs get here."

"I'm fine," I argued.

Kerry, who'd seen combat and had been wounded, kept his calm demeanor. "You were unconscious for a while. You probably have at least a concussion. Don't try to get up."

Having uttered similar calming words to badly wounded Marines, I suspected my trauma might be worse than I was feeling.

"Can you move your fingers and toes?" Kerry asked.

"Yes," I replied, flexing my fingers. "How long until the ambulance arrives?"

"They'll be here in a minute or two. Stay still until they get a cervical collar on you."

"Are they taking me to Duluth?"

"Actually, you're getting a helicopter ride to Duluth."

"I hate helicopters. They give me flashbacks to Iraq."

Kerry chuckled. "I'll warn them that they need to strap your arms down."

Grimacing as a wave of pain swept over my chest, I looked up at Kerry. "You just can't help yourself, can you? You've got to be a smartass even in the direst situations."

"That's not true. I was totally serious and concerned when Sparky was checking for a pulse."

"Did my heart actually stop?"

"I doubt it. Sparky overreacted when you passed out. He was ready to start chest compressions if he didn't find a pulse."

"What happened in the alley? I saw a flash?"

"Did your life pass before your eyes?" Sparky asked.

"No! Something flashed in the alley, and it felt like there had been an explosion."

"I think the arsonist poured gas into a dumpster full of cardboard. He's probably missing his eyebrows or more."

"I thought I tackled the arsonist?" I said.

"We're not sure who you tackled, but she wasn't the one who lit the fire."

"Is the exercise club on fire?"

Kerry shook his head. "Nope, just the dumpster in the alley."

The ambulance's arrival was signaled by an additional set of flashing lights reflecting off the downtown store windows. Kerry stood to make room for the EMTs.

"Wait!" I protested. "What happened to the person I tackled? Is he in worse shape than me?"

After a chuckle, Kerry leaned close. "She looks like the loser in a cat fight."

I totally missed Kerry's use of a female pronoun to describe the person I'd run into. "Why?"

"Didn't you notice Wendy's long fingernails? Her only move, other than sitting on top of the woman, was to scratch the hell out of her."

"Did he or Wendy get hurt?"

"I'm sure Wendy has some bruises from the encounter, but she wasn't the loser in that fight."

"Did you arrest him?"

The left side of Kerry's face was scarred from an IED explosion in Iraq. The right side grinned at me. "I arrested *her* for assault. The person who flattened you was a woman."

The eerie grin made my garbled mind uneasy. "Her? For assaulting who?"

"The person who decked you was a woman. Just before nailing you, Wendy saw her lower her shoulder as if she was trying to muscle you aside."

"The person who ran into me was a woman?"

"Don't worry, your macho image is still intact. Your assailant outweighed you by about thirty pounds. She plays in a Minnesota coed rugby league and was better prepared for the impact than you were."

It's funny how your mind bounces around when your head has been smashed against the sidewalk. Random thoughts about rugby flashed until I pictured a bumper sticker I'd seen years ago. *It takes leather balls to play rugby.* The image disappeared as quickly as it had arrived. "Coed rugby is a thing?"

Chuckling, Kerry replied, "Apparently. If it's any consolation, she was scrappy and ready to take me on. I had to use my taser on her before I put her in handcuffs."

The EMTs pushed Kerry aside. One put my neck in a cushioned collar while the other triaged my injuries. After asking me my name, the day of the week, whether I could move my fingers and toes, and who was my next of kin, they loaded me onto a gurney and wheeled me to the ambulance.

"Call Jenny!" I yelled to Kerry before the ambulance door closed.

"She's already on her way to Duluth!"

"The kids..."

"Deb is already at your house. It's all under control."

Chapter 22

I was in the ER for hours. After blood sampling, x-rays, and concussion testing protocol, they let Jenny see me. She hugged me, then leaned back. "The left side of your face looks like hamburger. What happened?"

"I was kind of out of it. I assume my left side was against the sidewalk while Wendy and the arsonist wrestled on top of me."

"Ah."

"That's it? 'Ah?'" I asked.

"HIPAA rules prevent the hospital staff from revealing the extent or nature of a patient's injuries."

"But you're my wife!"

"I didn't have any ID, so the receptionist was reluctant to let me see you until Kerry showed up and assured her that I was a relative."

"I heard the arsonist was scratched up."

"I think Wendy's manicurist is going to advertise the strength of her nail extensions based on what they did to the arsonist. Wendy never broke a single nail."

"I don't find that reassuring." A thought flickered, then left my brain. A moment later it was back. "Who was the arsonist?"

"You mean the alleged arsonist."

"Who did we catch and did Kerry find enough evidence to arrest him?"

"Her."

I turned my head to look at Jenny, which made me realize I had double vision from my head injury. "Her?" I asked, having a vague recollection of a rugby conversation with Kerry.

"Kat Devlin was the person who fought with Wendy."

"I don't know Kat Devlin."

"She's from Brimson. According to Kerry, she's got a long criminal record that ranges from petty theft to assault and battery. By the way, Kerry needs you to file a report about her assault on you."

"She didn't assault me as much as run into me and knock me down."

"Apparently, her running into you, then sitting on your head while she fought off Wendy, amounts to assault. She's the cause of the abrasions on the left side of your face and the contusions on the right side."

"I have contusions on the right side of my face?"

"The rivets in her jeans cut you up pretty badly while she squirmed around fighting with Wendy."

"It felt like I had an elephant sitting on me."

"Neither Kat nor Wendy are small women."

"Wait. Sparky was there, too. Is he okay?"

"Sparky had the good sense to stay out of the fight until Kat got tired of fending off Wendy's nails. Kerry zapped Kat with a taser before he dragged her off your head."

"Did Kerry arrest Wendy, too?"

"Why would he arrest Wendy?'

"It sounds like Wendy scratched the hell out of the woman."

Jenny laughed. "Talking to you is free association. I say something, then you're off in an unrelated discussion."

"We're still talking about Wendy. By the way, she has a cupid tattoo."

"I think you're delusional."

"I got a glimpse of it when she showed it to Sparky."

"Shh. Even if you did see Wendy's cupid tattoo, and I'm not sure you're imagining it, I don't need to know its location."

"Why would anyone get a tattoo on their..."

"Shh. No more tattoo discussions."

"Okay. Did Kerry arrest the woman for arson?"

"She isn't the arsonist."

"But she ran away when we confronted her."

"You fell for the diversion. She ran while her partner lit a fire."

I closed my eyes, trying to remember seeing a second person in the alley. "I only saw one person, but Wendy distracted me while we were crossing the street."

"And you called Kerry for backup."

"How bad was the fire?"

"The arsonist never got inside the building. Because of the commotion, he tipped over his gas can and lit the puddle in the alley. The fire department doused the flames before they did anything but light a fire in a dumpster behind The Body Shop."

"Did Kerry catch the arsonist?"

"No, but the firemen saw his car driving away. They radioed a description of the car to Kerry, who relayed it to the sheriff's department and state patrol. A trooper pulled the car over near Beaver Bay. He arrested the driver who smelled like gasoline and smoke. The car has been impounded."

"You got all this information from Kerry?"

"Are you kidding? Kerry is completely professional and doesn't share information like that. Sparky was telling anyone who'd listen that his firemen solved the crime."

* * *

With the sun rising, Jenny drove me home from the hospital. Thoughts and memories swirled in my head. Some nugget of information connected the previous evening's events, but I couldn't recall or connect it.

Deb Stone met us at the door, looking as tired as I felt. I showered while Jenny thanked Deb, then fed Jeremy and Amy breakfast. I sat on the edge of the bed, trying to focus, both visually and mentally. The red numerals on the alarm clock didn't align in my double vision, leaving me with the feeling I was failing an eye examination. The numbers jumped around until a five changed to a six. The unexpected change caused a wave of nausea.

Hearing my retching, Jenny rushed upstairs. I was leaning against the bathtub when she stepped into the bathroom. "Are you okay?" She asked as she knelt next to me and ran her fingers through my hair."

"I have to drive to Whistling Pines."

She snorted. "Your driving privileges are revoked until your double vision clears."

"But I need to talk to someone."

"You need to rest, honey."

Struggling to my feet, I used the towel bar to steady myself. "Call Kerry. I know who set the fires."

Wrapping her arm around my shoulders, Jenny guided me out of the bathroom. "You can talk to him later. You need to rest."

"No. If I fall asleep this thought will be gone. Dial Kerry's cell phone."

With me safely sitting on the edge of the bed and not in danger of falling down, or heaven forbid, driving, Jenny punched Kerry's number into the phone. "Hi Kerry, Peter asked me to call you. Here he is."

"Deb told me you were home," Kerry said, sounding as tired as I felt.

"Listen. The arsonists you arrested didn't set the fires back in the '60s and '70s."

Kerry chuckled. "That's pretty obvious. The guy wasn't born until 1999 and the woman was born in 2002."

"You don't understand, Kerry. I KNOW who set the old fires."

"Enlighten me, oh person with the concussion who has sudden visions of historical events. Did your Ouija board give you the answer, or are you using Tarot cards?"

"I'm serious, Kerry. He told us he was the arsonist."

"I must've slept through that discussion. Who were we talking to when he made this admission?"

As quickly as my vision of the discussion had appeared, it disappeared. "I can't remember his name. He lives at Whistling Pines."

"The arsonist lives at Whistling Pines, and he admitted that he'd set the fires in the '60s and '70s?"

"Yes. Pick me up and we can confront him."

"I'll tell you what. Since we know it's a man, and that he's a resident at Whistling Pines, let's both get some sleep. We'll figure out who it is, and I'll interview him this afternoon. Okay?"

"But?"

"Nothing is likely to change between now and this afternoon. If he's a resident of Whistling Pines, I doubt that he's a flight risk. Get some sleep and call me when you wake up."

Kerry disconnected the call, and I looked up at Jenny, who had been listening to the conversation. "He wants to talk after I get some sleep."

Jenny took the phone from my hand and plugged it into the charger on the nightstand. "I think that's a good plan."

"I'm not sure I can sleep."

Jenny gently eased my shoulders back until I was lying on the pillow, then pulled up the covers. "Close your eyes and see what happens."

"Did I tell you that Wendy has a cupid tattoo?"

"Shh. I don't want to know about Wendy's cupid tattoo. Go to sleep."

The last thing I remembered was Jeremy announcing that he was leaving to catch the school bus.

* * *

I awoke to the setting sun leaking in around the edges of the bedroom blinds. A glance at the alarm clock revealed that my double vision had cleared during my day-long nap. Easing myself out of bed, I determined that my legs were rubbery, but supported me adequately to attempt a shower. The combination of hot water pounding on my back and swirling steam refreshed me and brought back images of the chase that had ended with me under a pile of people. I tried to recall why I needed to speak with Kerry, but only succeeded in refreshing my memory of Wendy jumping into the back seat of my car. A flash of a cupid tattoo stuck in my mind. I tried to recall its exact location until reason returned and I banished the thought in favor of recalling who'd spoken to me about the historical arson fires.

A face came to mind, followed by a name, Darrell Sanders. Rushing to the bedroom, I unplugged my cell phone from the charger and dialed Kerry's number.

"Hi, Sleeping Beauty. How's your head?" Kerry said, chuckling.

"I remembered the arsonist's name. I think it's Darrell Sanders."

"Darrell, as in the father of the guy who owns The Body Shop?"

"Yes! We had a discussion one afternoon and he was disgusted by the new arsonist and virtually said that he had lit the historical fires."

"Back up. Did he make an admission to you, or did he hint at his involvement?"

"He knew about all the old fires, and he explained how they'd been started so it appeared they'd been accidental."

"That's what we cops call very thin circumstantial evidence."

"But he knew the details! Only the person who set the fires would know how the smoldering pile of sawdust had set the old lumberyard on fire."

"Was Darrell one of the volunteer firemen who responded to the arson fires?"

"Yes!"

"Settle down, Peter. Is it possible that he and his firehall buddies discussed the fires and came up with plausible ways the fires had been set?"

I sat down on the edge of the bed. "I think he had too much detail. And he was irritated that the bait shop fire was being lumped with the old arson fires. He said the new arsonist was an amateur. It was stated in a way that projected pride in the artistry of the historical arson fires. The arsonist is Darrell Sanders, Kerry. I'm sure of it."

"Tonight, is our Lutheran men's club poker game. Come to the game and we can bounce your thoughts off the other players while we drink coffee and play cards."

"I think we should confront Darrell and see if he admits to being the arsonist."

Kerry's pause was lengthy. "That only works on TV cop shows. Criminals are unwilling to unburden their consciences to cops under questioning. We need a different plan."

"Put a wire on me and I'll talk to Darrell. I'm sure I can get him to admit he lit those fires."

"Take it easy, Peter. If I heard you correctly, he didn't *admit* his involvement in those fires. He just left you with the impression that he knew too much."

"But Kerry..."

"Listen, Peter, let's think this through. Barging in and demanding a confession from someone has never proven an effective way of extracting a confession from someone. Let's talk about it with the poker group and a strategy may emerge. If nothing else, you can see if the other three guys agree with me about not confronting the alleged arsonist."

Hearing the kitchen door and the sound of voices in the kitchen, I gave up my argument. "Fine. I think Jenny just walked into the house. I'll tell her I'm going to the poker game and sneak away."

"Can you drive? If you're still having double vision, you shouldn't be behind the wheel."

"My double vision is pretty much gone."

"Um, *pretty much gone* doesn't fill me with confidence. I'll pick you up in half an hour."

"I can drive myself," I replied to the dial tone.

The aroma of burgers and fries greeted my nose as I walked downstairs. Jeremy was pulling wrapped hamburgers out of bags as Jenny strapped Amy into her highchair. Being the only one who noticed me, Amy started flapping her arms with joy when I appeared in the dining room.

Reacting to Amy's happy gesture, Jenny looked over her shoulder. "Did we wake you?"

I sat across from Jeremy who was squirting ketchup onto a burger wrapper. "I woke up a few minutes ago. I was on the phone with Kerry when I heard you come in."

After securing the last of the highchair straps, Jenny turned and pecked me on the cheek. "I brought supper home. Jeremy wanted burgers and fries. We can split the

Cobb salad in the second bag if you'd like some."

I took a burger from the pile Jeremy had created on the table and peeled back the wrapper. "I'm not terribly hungry. I think a burger and a few fries will fill me up."

"How's your head?" Jenny asked as she opened the plastic container with the salad and squirted dressing on top of it.

"My head is better. I only see one of you."

"Just because your double vision has cleared, doesn't mean that your concussion has healed. You might have headaches and memory issues for weeks."

"Thanks for that happy bit of information," I replied as I bit into a burger.

"I'm just repeating what the ER nurse told you when she read your discharge instructions."

"I don't remember anyone saying anything about my memory or headaches."

Jenny stopped with a forkful of salad halfway to her mouth. "I rest my case. The discharge papers are on the kitchen table if you'd care to see just what you are and aren't supposed to do for the next day and week."

"I might prefer to ignore them."

"For a guy who used to be a Navy corpsman, you're pretty calloused about medical orders."

"The Marines I treated went back to their units as soon as they were released from the hospital. They didn't hang around the base for a week waiting for their headaches to stop."

"First of all, you're not a Marine. Secondly, this is not Iraq and there's no squad depending on you. Thirdly, you're married to a healthcare professional who will have the police chief handcuff you to the bed if you don't follow the doctor's orders."

I smiled. "Kerry won't handcuff me to the bed."

"If he won't, I'm sure his wife will."

I was about to make a remark about being handcuffed to a bed being kind of kinky when I realized that Jeremy was listening carefully to our conversation. "I was just kidding with your mom," I said. "I'm going to follow the doctor's orders and do exactly what she tells me I should do to heal."

Jeremy shrugged and dove into a pile of fries. I felt Jenny's hand on my arm. "Thank you, Daddy."

I nodded. "I'm a little new to this job of modeling adult behavior."

"You're catching on."

"Kerry is going to pick me up. We're going to Pastor Olafson's veteran's group meeting."

"Do you feel up to playing cards and drinking coffee?" Jenny asked.

"Kerry suggested I share a conversation I had with Darrell Sanders with that group."

"What did Darrell tell you?"

"He had amazingly detailed thoughts on how the historical arson fires had been set so they looked accidental. He was also very upset that the bait shop fire was being lumped in with those older arson fires. He claims that the new arsonist is an amateur."

Jenny stopped eating. "Why would he tell you that?"

I made sure Jeremy was absorbed by his dinner and ignoring our conversation, then said, "I think the historical arsonist considers himself somewhat of an artist. He wants it understood that the new arsonist is not as skilled in the art."

"Did you tell Kerry?"

I nodded as I snatched a couple of fries from Jeremy's pile. "I did. He suggested that we run my observations past the other men's club members to see if there's some way of exposing the old arsonist."

Kerry's knock on the door interrupted our discussion. Standing, I pecked Jenny on the cheek. "I've got to run."

Kerry peeked into the dining room. "Is it okay for me to kidnap your husband for a couple of hours?"

Jenny flipped her fingers, signaling her wish for me to leave. "Please bring him back sober and try to keep him from reinjuring his head."

"How would he reinjure his head playing cards with the men's club?" Kerry asked, handing my jacket to me.

"There seems to be no end to the ways you two find trouble."

Kerry frowned. "Deb thinks that Peter keeps me out of trouble."

Rolling her eyes, Jenny sighed. "You're either stretching the truth or Deb is extremely naïve."

"Deb thinks my judgement is sometimes lacking, and that Peter tempers poor decisions I might make."

"Yeah, you two are just like Adam Sandler and Jim Carrey. I'm not sure the two of you should be left unsupervised."

"I'll have him home before 10:00."

Chapter 23

There were three vehicles in the church parking lot when we arrived. Pastor Olafson shuffled the cards as Kevin counted out piles of poker chips and I hung my coat behind the office door. Augie pulled out a chair for me when I approached the table and paid my two dollars for my pile of chips. "Nice road rash, Doc. It looks like your motorcycle crashed."

Reflexively touching my abraded cheek, I took the chair and smiled. "There was no motorcycle involved, just a large arsonist who sat on my head."

"That's the problem with you Navy corpsmen, you never learned how to not be at the bottom of the pile during a fight. The Marines taught us we should be on top of the person we're fighting."

Kerry chuckled. "Worse yet, the two people wrestling on top of him were both women."

That comment caught Kevin's attention. "That sounds kind of kinky. Two women on top with you on the bottom. This discussion may be inappropriate for the pastor's office."

Trying to change the topic, Pastor Olafson dealt the cards. "Seven-card stud. Shut up and make your bets."

Augie pulled a bottle of bourbon from his jacket pocket and poured generous dollops of booze into the half-full coffee cups that Kevin had placed in front of us.

"Take it easy Augie," Kevin said. "I have to drive the state pickup home and it'd look bad if the police chief ticketed me for a DWI."

Augie laughed. "I only put two glugs of booze in each mug, and the police chief will have the same blood alcohol level as you do."

The pastor took a sip of his coffee. "Is a 'glug' a quantitative measure, Augie?"

"Sure. Haven't you ever put a couple glugs of gas into your lawnmower? It's just the right amount to get you going but not so much that you spill over the top."

Olafson grinned and said, "Peter has a king showing. He bets."

Looking at the others' cards that didn't match each other or the king, I threw one white chip into the middle. "I bet one cent."

The game went on, each of us kidding the others about something. The piles of chips in front of us grew and shrunk, but never went entirely away. No one cared. More coffee and bourbon were dispensed, and the laughter grew louder.

After folding a terrible hand, Kerry leaned back. "Peter has something to run past you guys."

Having won the hand with a pair of jacks, Augie collected the chips and shuffled the cards. "How could this group of reprobates possibly be helpful to you, Peter?"

Explaining the conversation with Darrell Sanders and the recent bait shop fire, I threw out the question, "How do we get Darrell to admit that he's the arsonist?"

Kevin threw one white chip into the kitty. "Ante is one chip for whatever game Augie chooses as he cheats us out of our chips." As the chips flew into the middle, Kevin said, "It's impossible to get someone reasonably smart to admit to a crime. You need to have a discussion with him without a cop, like Kerry or me, around. I think you might have a chance to get him to admit lighting the fires if you stroke his ego a bit, then start talking about how the bait shop fire arsonist is so smart that he made the fire appear like the person who set the old fires wasn't as smart as this new arsonist."

"I don't see what you're saying," I replied.

"Tell him that the lumberyard fire was genius. Say the same about the details of the other older fires you know about. Then, explain how the new arsonist was extremely smart by making the bait shop fire look like it was set by a rank amateur. 'Gee, this new fire was so different from the old fires that no one would ever suspect that the same person set it. The arsonist was a genius, changing his technique to make people believe that someone different set it.'"

Nodding, I mulled Kevin's comments. "Darrell seemed proud of the way the old fires had been set so they looked accidental. He might get so angry over me saying the new fire

270

was smart, he might be angry enough to set me straight.”

The pastor shook his head. “Or you might anger him, and he’ll burn your house down.”

Augie smiled. “I agree. There’s a definite downside to pissing off an arsonist.”

Kerry, deep in thought, was tapping a chip on the table. “That’s it. Peter pisses him off and the old arsonist has to light a fire to prove he’s smarter than the new guy and the cops.”

Augie dealt cards and nodded. “The key is finding a target that’s so tempting for the arsonist that you know where he’s going to set the fire, then you can catch him in the act.”

Kerry grinned at me. “Great idea, Augie. We can set up surveillance on the site and catch him. Peter and Sparky are a great surveillance team.”

I glowered at Kerry, but Augie was on a roll. “Anderson’s hardware store is having a clearance sale, then going out of business for good. If word gets around that old man Anderson is going bankrupt and needs the money from the building, the arsonist might feel like it’s his civic duty to help him out by burning down the store.”

I leaned back. “That’s fine, but how do we do that without allowing the store to burn down?”

Kerry’s eyes lit up. “We have three or four firemen with extinguishers inside the store. They can deal with whatever the arsonist does.”

"Just to be clear," I said, "I will NOT be one of the people inside the store."

Kerry patted my shoulder. "No, you and Sparky will be the people who get Darrell all riled up so he needs to demonstrate what a smart arsonist he is compared to the amateur."

"I'm not much of an actor."

Augie raised his eyebrows. "Sparky is a great improvisational actor. Think back to his television interview and the 'no newts' protest. He diverted the whole protest discussion away from the minister's daughter posing nude. Sparky can think on his feet."

The pastor shook his head. "To be fair, Sparky's lived with his mother and hasn't dated much. He's...socially inept."

Kerry stood and walked into the hallway, taking his cell phone out of his pocket as he left. "I'll call Sparky."

"And tell him what?" I asked as he closed the door.

Kevin scooped up the cards and shuffled. "I think he's making plans for the two of you to get Darrell Sanders wound up."

"Great," I said, holding my cup out to Augie. "I think I need a couple more glugs of bourbon."

Kerry returned smiling. "Sparky is excited. He's going to meet you in your office tomorrow morning."

"That's just great," I replied, without meaning to say it out loud.

* * *

As promised, Sparky was standing outside my office when I arrived. I wasn't sure if my headache was related to my concussion or the extra bourbon I'd consumed. Either way, I was unprepared for Sparky's enthusiasm.

"So, we're really going to do this?" he asked as I unlocked my office.

"Easy, Sparky. We need this to be a credible, soft sell."

Sitting in my visitor chair while I hung my jacket behind the door, Sparky asked, "How are we going to do that? I mean, do you have a script? Do I have to memorize lines?"

"We need to sound spontaneous. I think scripting our discussion would make it sound pre-rehearsed and stilted."

"Got it. We're going to ad lib like they do on that television show *Whose Line is It Anyway?*"

"Something like that. Our objective is to guide Sanders toward making a rash decision. We're not trying for laughs."

"Right. I can be serious as hell. Like when I was talking to the news people about the Norwegian newts. I thought that was pretty smart of me. I totally diverted them from the issue of the nude modeling protest."

"As much as it pains me to say so, you did a pretty good job of that interview. None of the news people had a clue about the nude modeling until the next day."

"How are we going to do this? Are we going to sit down with him and tell him he needs to light one more fire so we can bust him for all the historical arson fires?"

I closed the office door and sat down. "I think an indirect approach would be best. Let's sit down at a table near where he's seated and have a discussion about how brilliant the new arsonist is."

"I thought the bait shop arsonist was an idiot."

"That's what Sanders thinks, too. If we talk about how smart the new guy was to light a fire that looked like a rookie did it, I think Darrell will have to prove us wrong."

Sparky nodded. "Okay. Should we talk about other stuff too?"

"The key will be to make our conversation sound natural. So, yes, we should just be talking about other things, then let the conversation drift to the bait shop fire."

Sparky stood. "Let's do it!"

I led Sparky to the dining room and filled mugs of coffee for us. To his credit, Sparky appeared totally at ease. "If the Vikings traded for another decent wide receiver, I think they could make a run for the division championship."

"Really?"

"They don't have a chance once they get into the playoffs, but I think they could win enough games to be ahead of Green Bay, Chicago, and Detroit."

I led Sparky to a table with two empty chairs where Howard Johnson and Lee Westfall were seated. Darrell Sanders was sitting at the next table with his back to Howard. "May we join you?" I asked.

Always the gentleman, Howard gestured to the empty chairs. "We're always happy to have visitors."

Lee nodded. "It's been pretty quiet around here lately. Can you two stir up some controversy? I enjoy listening to a good argument."

"I don't know if you two know the Two Harbors Fire Chief. Sparky, these gentlemen are Howard Johnson and Lee Westfall."

Sparky shook hands and sat next to Lee. "I'm not very argumentative. I was just commenting on the Vikings chances of getting into the playoffs."

Lee shrugged. "I'm more into Iowa college football than the Vikings."

Howard chuckled, "The Vikings couldn't make the playoffs if they played the Minneapolis school for talented artistic children."

"Ooh," Sparky said. "That's quite a burn."

Lee's expression changed. "Are you the guy Wendy's been dating?"

"I am!" Sparky replied.

Lee laughed. "I hear you're quite a gentleman."

"I try to be."

Lee started laughing. "If you're going to make it with Wendy, I think you need to be more of a bad boy. She seems to like her dates to be a bit shady and daring."

"She showed up in the back seat of Peter's car during a stakeout. I think that's kind of shady and daring."

"That was Wendy being daring? You were there to watch for the arsonist," I said.

"What were you staking out?" Lee asked.

"We were watching a building where we thought an arsonist was going to strike," Sparky explained.

"Were you at that hardware store that's going bankrupt?" Lee asked.

"No, we had a tip that someone was going to burn down The Body Shop."

I noticed Darrell Sanders tilt his head slightly to better hear our discussion and decided to try and set the hook. "After the bait shop fire, we had a tip that the arsonist was going to light a fire downtown, so we staked out a different building, although the bankrupt hardware store would seem like an obvious target for someone trying to collect insurance money."

"Did you catch him?" Lee asked.

"We caught his girlfriend," I explained. "The arsonist was too smart. It's like the bait shop fire. He was really smart about making the scene look like a stupid teenager had dumped gas, lit it, and run away. We talked to the state arson investigator, and he thinks the arsonist was very cagey in setting the scene. He speculated that the guy was even smarter than the person who set the fires back in the '60s and '70s."

"Really?" Howard asked.

Sparky was getting into the role. "Yup. That old-time arsonist was pretty good, but this new guy is even smarter. Either that, or he's so stupid that he looks good. Either way, we're having a hard time figuring out how he set the bait shop fire without torching himself."

Darrell Sanders stood abruptly, bumping into the back of Howard's chair. "That guy is a hack," he said, before stomping off.

Howard glared over his shoulder at Sanders as he walked away. "I wonder what's bugging him?"

"Probably something he ate," Sparky suggested.

Lee leaned close to Sparky. "Did you and Wendy get close to second base on your last date?"

Sparky smiled. "I almost made a hat trick with her last night."

Howard and I glanced at each other. "You and Wendy had three romantic interludes in one evening?" Howard asked.

Sparky snorted. "No. I almost made it to third base at the ice arena."

Howard couldn't contain his laughter. "At the ice arena?"

Sparky became serious. "It's not easy finding places for romance when you live with your mother. And Wendy kind of likes being spontaneous."

"How did you get into the ice arena?" Lee asked.

Sparky reached down and lifted a ring with dozens of keys. "The fire department has keys to every public building in town. You know, in case of a fire. No one wants to wait until somebody unlocks the doors."

"What possessed you to choose the ice arena as compared to...the library?" Howard asked. "I'd think the arena would be cold."

"I have library nightmares," Sparky whispered. "When I was a kid, the librarian stalked around rapping people over the head with a yardstick when she caught us whispering. I think that might induce performance anxiety, you know, if we ever got to that point in our relationship."

Intrigued, Lee frowned. "You don't think that the cold in the ice arena would cause certain other functional problems?"

Sparky frowned. "Like what?"

Howard laughed. "Think about what happens when you swim in Lake Superior."

Sparky shrugged. "I get cold."

"Think specifically about the part of you that might not perform if it was extremely cold."

Closing his eyes, Sparky nodded. "Cold water shrinkage. Darn."

Not wanting to get into a discussion of Sparky's body parts shrinking in cold water, I stood. "Let's go back to my office, Sparky."

"Do you think Sanders caught onto us?" Sparky whispered as we walked away.

"He seemed genuinely upset over your characterization of the bait shop arsonist as smart. I don't know if that will be enough to motivate him to set the record straight, but we made our best attempt."

"I was thinking about what Lee and Howard said about the ice arena and cold swimming pools. Can you think of anywhere that has a sauna or hot tub?"

"Sparky..."

"I'll figure something out."

I closed my office door and dialed Kerry's cell phone. "We put on our act for Darrell Sanders."

"Do you think he bought it?" Kerry asked.

"He stomped off mumbling about amateurs," I replied.

Sparky leaned close to the phone. "Hi Chief, this is Sparky. I think he took it hook, line, and sinker. Are we doing another stakeout tonight?"

Chapter 24

I picked up Sparky at the fire station at sunset. As before, he brought his metal lunch box and a thermos. Climbing in, he closed the door. "I brought two cups tonight."

"That's nice of you. I have a couple cans of soda, so I'm well set for the stakeout." I pulled away from the station and drove toward the old part of town where Anderson's hardware store overlooked a side street. "Wendy isn't joining us tonight, is she?"

"I think she had some girly things to do. She said something about a pedicure and nails."

Finding a spot in an alley across from the hardware store, we hunkered down as Mr. Anderson closed down for the night. As the lights went out, I saw motion in the rear of the store. "Are your firemen inside?"

"They took their positions a couple of hours ago so it wouldn't look suspicious if people walked in as the store closed."

"Good plan."

We watched Mr. Anderson drive away and slouched down in our seats. A moment later the aroma of a warm pasty filled the car. "Would you like a pasty?" Sparky asked, referring to the local favorite meat, carrot, rutabaga, and potato filling baked in a pie crust.

"You made pasties for the stakeout?"

"My mom made a pan of pasties, and they were just coming out of the oven when it was time to leave. She wrapped two in foil and put them in my dad's old lunch box. Do you want one?"

I reflected on the pastor's comments about Sparky living with his mother and his social ineptitude but was touched by his thoughtfulness in packing a second pasty for me. "I ate supper before I left home. I'll munch on some snacks later if I get hungry. But thanks for the offer."

Sparky was silent as he squeezed ketchup from a fast-food packet onto the pasty and took a bite from his foil-wrapped supper. "I guess I never thought much about the gas production potential in a rutabaga. Is that going to be a problem if we're trapped in the car together all night?" he asked as he squeezed more ketchup onto the pasty.

"I'll roll down the window if it bothers me," I replied.

"Do you want some hot cocoa? Mom filled the thermos and there's enough for both of us."

Marveling that Sparky could balance the pasty, ketchup packets, thermos, and cups on his lap and the car's dashboard, I said, "Sure, I'll take a cup of cocoa."

The thermos opened with a pop and the aroma of chocolate mingled with the smell of the pasty. My phone vibrated and I answered it as Sparky set a cup of steaming cocoa into my cupholder. I tried to shield the glowing screen from view outside the car. "Yeah?"

"Augie and Kevin are a block down from the store," Kerry reported. "They're in Augie's farm truck."

"You brought in more civilians?" I asked.

"They thought you and Sparky might need backup."

"Geez, Kerry. We've already got volunteer firemen inside the store, Sparky and me across the street, and now you've got a farmer and the conservation officer down the block. Doesn't it seem like overkill?"

"Hang on, I've got a call from Kevin coming in."

"What's up?" Sparky asked.

Covering the glowing cell phone screen I replied, "Chief Stone says the conservation officer and a friend of his are down the block in a farm pickup."

"Since you don't want the other pasty, why don't you call and ask if one of them wants it."

I looked at Sparky. "I think it would look suspicious if you carried a pasty to Augie's truck."

"Good point. Someone might see the light come on inside your car when I open the door."

"I think the bigger issue would be you running down the empty street carrying your lunch box. The arsonist might find that suspicious."

"I wore black jeans and a dark coat."

"True. But your white face kind of stands out."

"Oh. Good point. I'll just stay here."

Kerry returned to the call. "My part time officer just reported a car leaving the Whistling Pines parking lot with its headlights off. He couldn't see the license plate or tell how many people were inside."

"Is he following the car?" I asked.

"If it's Sanders, we already know he's driving toward the hardware store."

"What if he decides to torch something other than the hardware store?" I asked.

"I see him turning into the alley behind the hardware store right now."

I ended the call and turned to Sparky. "Put away your cocoa and pasty. It looks like our arsonist just turned into the alley behind the hardware store."

There was a metallic thud, then I saw a flash of metal as Sparky fumbled the thermos. That was followed by the sensation of warm liquid soaking my pants.

"Oh, heck. The thermos got away from me. Did any of the cocoa get on you?"

I dug a wad of paper napkins out of my armrest and tried to sop up hot liquid from my pants.

"Dang it!" Sparky cursed, "the pasty got away from me too!"

Something bounced off my shoulder and landed on my lap. I reached down to pick up the pasty, my fingers becoming covered in ketchup and chunks of meat and pie crust.

"Did that get on you, Doc? I'm sorry, let me wipe it up."

I grabbed Sparky's hand before he reached for the food laying on my crotch. "I've got it, Sparky."

"I'm really sorry. I got kind of excited."

My phone vibrated somewhere in the mess of cocoa, ketchup, and pasty filling. The screen lit and I wiped ketchup off the front of it onto my jacket. "Yeah."

"We've got flames in the back of the store. Block the north end of the alley."

Starting the engine, I pulled out of our hiding spot and onto the empty street as Sparky grabbed his cocoa in one hand and the remaining pasty in the other. A half block down, I turned right, then stopped crosswise in the alley as a car without headlights raced towards us.

Throwing the pasty, ketchup and cocoa cup onto the floorboards, Sparky yelled, "Doc, he's going to hit my door!" He twisted in his seat, then started to climb into the backseat behind me.

Tires screeched as the approaching car braked. Then it veered to the right, colliding with a dumpster sitting behind a restaurant. I was out of my car, ready to chase, or save the driver as the dumpster flipped over, spewing garbage all over the alley, me, and the car. A second later, Sparky jumped out of the back door, slipping on the remnants of a spaghetti dinner. A family of racoons had apparently been in the dumpster, and they raced in different directions, making cat-like noises as they skittered away.

Picking himself up and wiping spaghetti sauce on his pants, Sparky said, "Holy mackerel, Doc! There's food all over the place."

Behind the arsonist's car, flames licked the back of the hardware store. The firemen who'd been hiding in the hardware store threw open the back door and directed clouds of fire extinguisher powder at the blaze. Sirens whined in the distance, and the flashing lights of Kerry's cruiser raced down the alley behind Augie's pickup.

As the vehicles stopped, the door of the crashed car opened, and Darrell Sanders stepped out. "Just what in hell do you guys think you're doing?" he asked Sparky and me.

"I think we just arrested the most elusive arsonist in the history of Two Harbors," I replied, as Kerry produced a pair of handcuffs.

* * *

After wiping garbage, cocoa, and ketchup from our clothing in the police station bathroom, Sparky and I spent most of the evening in Kerry's office, recording our statements, then signing the transcribed documents. At some point, Deb Stone showed up, commented on the stinking garbage staining my pants, then disappeared.

A few minutes later, Jenny arrived with a shopping bag. She held it out at arm's length. "Deb said you needed a change of clothes." Picking a piece of rutabaga from my hair, she added, "I think you'd better shower before you change."

Kerry showed me to the locker room with a shower in the back of the police station. He was waiting for me when I came out of the locker room with wet hair and dressed in clean clothes. "I think the garbage stink has permeated your skin. I hope you don't plan to be near anyone."

"I didn't do much except block the alley."

Kerry chuckled. "I doubt that you'll even get credit for that."

"What do you mean?"

"Sparky is outside being interviewed by a news broadcaster. According to his version of events, he single-handedly identified, stopped, and arrested the arsonist who's set half of Two Harbors aflame over the past half century."

"Good for him! I have no interest in being credited with anything but going home with my wife."

Augie and Kevin were in Kerry's office drinking coffee with Jenny. They all looked up when we walked in. Augie sniffed the air. "My manure compost pile smells better than you, Peter."

"Your compost pile probably wasn't covered by a hot pasty and cocoa when the fire chief got overly excited."

Kevin held his nose. "I think it's the combination of pasty, cocoa, and the day-old garbage that has penetrated your skin. Please stand farther away from me."

Moving away from Augie, I protested, "Kevin, you're the conservation officer who deals with roadkill and dead carcasses all the time."

"I've got to say, a roadkill beaver smells better than you do right now."

Jenny nodded. "I think a maggot would gag if it smelled you right now."

"I can't imagine Sparky smells any better than I do."

Kerry nodded. "The poor broadcaster who's interviewing him is stifling her gag reflex and has tears streaming down her face. I don't think they're tears of emotion. I think the dumpster stink is making her eyes water." He gestured for us to leave. "Go home before I need to fumigate my office."

I walked out with Jenny, who held my hand. "Kerry said you and Sparky pulled off the biggest arson bust in northern Minnesota history."

"I'll be glad to go back to my quiet life as a recreation director."

A roaring car engine screamed toward us, then braked nearly in front of the police station. Wendy jumped out and raced to Sparky, who was just ending his interview with the broadcaster. Virtually throwing herself at Sparky, Wendy hugged him, then ran her fingers through his hair to remove the remnants of what appeared to be a corned beef and cabbage dinner.

Jenny looked at me. "I think she's in love."

"Sparky still doesn't have a clue what he's gotten himself into," I replied.

"I remember a sailor who had the same problem. It seems like he figured it out."

"I wasn't as clueless as Sparky!"

Jenny stopped next to the car. Resisting the urge to hug me, she held me at arm's length. "You were worse."

* * *

Kerry knocked on the back door while we were eating breakfast. His face was ashen and his eyes bloodshot, like he hadn't slept. "You look like you need a cup of coffee," I said, holding the door for him.

Hearing Jeremy and Jenny talking in the dining room, he glanced past me. "Let's take a couple of cups to my car where we can talk without being overheard."

Sitting beside him, I watched as he stared at the travel mug I'd filled for him. "Are you okay?"

"Not entirely," he replied before taking a sip of coffee. "It's been a long night and I unearthed things that were better left buried."

"I don't understand."

"The Sanders family had an arson business going back to the early twentieth century. Darrell learned how to set fires from his father, who'd been taught by Darrell's grandfather."

"Three generations of firebugs."

"It was more than that. Darrell framed their arson as a public service business. As we'd surmised, all the buildings that burned down had been having financial problems. The Sanders family were upstanding citizens by day but were also known as the people who could take care of your problem buildings if you were having trouble making ends meet."

"Are you saying the arson business wasn't a secret?"

"To hear Darrell tell it, they were like Batman or Robin Hood, just common people who came forward to help the underdogs when they were needed."

"He admitted to setting several fires?"

Kerry shook his head. "Darrell was very canny. He spoke in generalities about the arson history of Two Harbors, pinning the blame on family members who were dead. He didn't admit to anything."

"He was pretty worked up when we talked about how smart the bait shop arsonist was."

"Yeah, he viewed the bait shop fire as an amateur job, not in the same league as the professional arsons performed by his family."

"Did you arrest him?"

Kerry sipped his coffee and shook his head. "I've got nothing to connect him to anything but the fire at the hardware store, and he swears that was an accident."

"How was that an accident? He was there when the fire started."

"A bunch of towels soaked with linseed oil were thrown near the back door. According to Darrell, they ignited spontaneously."

"And you believed him?"

"I spoke with Steve Zaccard, the state arson investigator. Linseed oil oxidizes as it cures. A linseed-soaked rag in a confined space can ignite spontaneously. They cause a number of shop fires every year."

"What are the odds that a linseed-soaked rag would happen to ignite as Darrell Sanders drove past the back of the hardware store?"

"The standard for convicting someone of a felony is guilt beyond reasonable doubt. There's no way the county attorney is going to risk his political career by prosecuting a case where there's obvious doubt."

"Kerry, Sanders is going to get away with arson!"

"Haven't I ever explained the theory of incarcerated criminals to you?"

"If you did, I wasn't paying attention."

"There are two groups of criminals in prison. One group are the dumb ones, who are caught easily. The other group are the ones who were unlucky enough to get caught red handed. If you ask any individual criminal which group he's in, he'll reply that he's one of the unlucky few."

"What are you telling me?"

"Darrell's family was smart. And smart criminals don't get caught unless they mess up and do something dumb or have the bad luck to be lighting a fire when a cop or fireman walks past."

"He's going to get away with it," I said, squeezing my cup as if I wanted to strangle it.

"I'm afraid so."

"There must be some way to link him to the crime. Did he have a can of linseed oil in his car, or was one of the rags a shirt marked with his initials?"

"The rags were white cotton t-shirts you could buy anywhere. They were soaked with linseed oil somewhere else and transported to the scene in Ziplock bags. The bags burned up in the fire, so there aren't any fingerprints to recover. The arsonist was very smart, and just quick enough so no one actually saw him throw the rags out, nor did they see Darrell light the fire."

"I thought the linseed ignited by itself."

"It does, given enough time. Darrell didn't have the luxury of time, so it appears he lit the rags with a disposable lighter that he threw into the pile of flaming rags before he drove away."

"You're telling me that the inside of my car is soaked with pasty and cocoa for no good reason."

"That's not entirely true. I'm sure Darrell's family arson career is over." Kerry paused. "And we caught the bait shop arsonist."

"How?"

"When the county attorney charged the woman you tackled with being an accessory to murder for the bait shop fire, she talked to her public defender and they worked out a plea deal. She turned over her slimeball boyfriend in return for a suspended sentence and probation."

"Who was the arsonist? Did he kill Antonich by accident?"

"Antonich's nephew had some financial setbacks in the housing crash of the early 2000s. He's been limping along as a realtor, waiting for the windfall he was going to get from selling Stanley Cup championship rings when his childless uncle died."

"And he got tired of waiting," I said.

"He hired a guy who was advertising on one of those 'invisible' internet sites where illegal activities and prostitution are offered."

"Why didn't the nephew have the arsonist kill Antonich at his home?"

"He didn't want to risk losing or melting Antonich's championship rings. The nephew had no idea how well off Speedy was. He assumed that selling off the rings would be a big enough payday to cover his debts. Speedy's humble lifestyle led the nephew to believe the only real assets Antonich had were the rings."

"So, the girlfriend threw the arsonist and Antonich's nephew under the bus?"

Kerry chuckled. "We also have Sanders to thank for that. He was so incensed by the bait shop fire being lumped in with his family's *professional* arson fires, that he hired the internet arsonist to start a fire at The Body Shop. Then he tipped you off to the upcoming fire so you would alert me, we'd set up a sting, and the internet arsonist would be arrested."

"And we blew it because Wendy turned on the overhead light in my backseat. He saw the light inside my car and panicked."

"Yup. You, Sparky, and Wendy turned out to be the most inept surveillance team in history. You saw just enough of what was happening to stop the fire from damaging the business. But you tipped the arsonist off before you could call in the cavalry to make the arrest."

"We caught the girlfriend, but not the arsonist," I groaned.

"Exactly. You were chasing the gecko and caught the tail that broke off while the body of the gecko got free."

"But you can arrest Darrell for hiring the arsonist for The Body Shop fire, right?"

"I assume it was Darrel, but the transaction was conducted over the internet and there's nothing but circumstantial evidence tying him to the crime."

I reached for the door handle, "Well, thanks for clearing up the mystery. I'm happy that Sparky, Wendy, and I were so inept that our services will no longer be required."

"Don't get your hopes up, sailor boy. You're still my best local resource."

"But we messed up two stakeouts."

"And solved a hundred years of arson fires in the process."

"Shit."

Kerry started laughing.

"It's not that funny."

"One other crime was averted early this morning."

"What would that be?"

"A silent alarm went off at the fire station."

"Did someone break in?"

"Not exactly. The perpetrator had a key."

"I'm lost."

"Sparky finally found a warm spot where Wendy could express her deep pride in his heroic efforts in stopping the arsonist. Everything was going to plan except Sparky got overly excited and forgot to disable the silent burglar alarm when they snuck into the fire station."

"You caught them making whoopee in the fire station?"

Kerry laughed. "Two county deputies, a state trooper, and I rushed the building with guns drawn, thinking that there was a burglary in progress."

"How embarrassing was it?" I asked,

"Wendy slid out of the back seat of the fire truck with her hands raised."

"So?"

"She was buck naked and laughing. Sparky covered his crotch with a fire helmet."

"Police induced coitus interruptus," I said, chuckling.

"No, they were past that point and into snuggling in the afterglow." Kerry paused.

"Did you know that Wendy has a little rainbow tattoo near her…"

"Yeah, I heard about the pot of gold at the end of the rainbow." I paused. "Did you arrest them?"

"Why would I do that? They're consenting adults. Sparky is the fire chief and has every right to be in the fire station. I suggested that he limit his future firehouse tours to daylight hours."

"Why are you telling me this?"

"I think Sparky's going to ask you to be his best man."

"What?"

"He's very traditional, and he apparently feels that making love to someone means that you have to marry them."

"I think that ship sailed a long time ago for Wendy."

Kerry grinned. "I have the impression that Sparky was a virgin until last night. Besides, he feels like it's time for him to move out of Mom's house. He's looking for a place to rent." Kerry pointed to the FOR RENT sign on the empty house next door to the driveway. "Maybe they'll move in next to you."

"Don't you dare suggest that. There's no way I want to live next door to Wendy and Sparky."

"Look! Is that Sparky's pickup pulling up in front of the rental?"

"That's not funny, Kerry."

With his eyes twinkling, Kerry said, "I think that would be divine justice."

The End

Dean L. Hovey mysteries from BWL Publishing Inc.

Whistling Pines cozies
Whistling up a Ghost
Whistling Pirates
Whistling Bake Off
Whistling Artist
Whistling Fireman

Doug Fletcher mysteries
Stolen Past
Washed Away
Dead in the Water
Death in Shifting Sands
Devils Fall
Prairie Menace
Down River
Burnt Evidence
Gator Bait
Grave Survey
Dead End Trail
The Last Rodeo
Peril in Paradise

Pine County Mysteries
Killer Secrets
Deadly Mixture
Fatal Business
Taxed to Death

Dean Hovey is the award-winning and best-selling author of three mystery series. He uses his scientific background, travel, extensive research, and consultants to add reality and depth to his stories. One reader said his characters are like people he'd like to invite over for a beer and discussion.

Hovey's Doug Fletcher mysteries follow U.S. National Park Service investigators Doug and Jill Fletcher as their investigations take them to national parks from coast to coast. The Whistling Pines mysteries are humorous cozies set in a northern Minnesota senior residence, following Peter Rogers, the Whistling Pines recreation director, as he stumbles through the investigation of murders in his small town. The Pine County mystery series follows sheriff's deputies Pam Ryan, Floyd Swenson, and C.J. Jensen as they investigate murders in rural Minnesota.

Dean and his wife split their year between northern Minnesota and Arizona.